PISTOLS AT DAWN

BESTSELLING AUTHOR
ANDREA PICKENS

One

A metallic click caused Marcus Fitzherbert Greeley, the Earl of Killingworth to look up from his ledgers.

"Who's there?" he called sharply.

No answer.

But after a moment, the draperies stirred and a dark shape emerged from the midnight shadows. As the cloaked figure approached his desk, candlelight glinted off the steel of an ancient pistol.

"Stand up," came the curt command.

The case clock ticked off a second or two before the earl put down his pen and rose.

"Take off your coat."

He didn't move, save for a slight twitch of his raven brows.

"You think a mere female incapable of pulling the trigger? I assure you, if you give me the slightest provocation I should like nothing better." The young lady—for her speech, if not her actions, indicated that she was indeed a lady—stepped closer. "And in case you are wondering, I am accorded to be a decent shot."

Marcus slowly shrugged out of the elegant navy superfine garment and let it drop to the Oriental carpet.

"Now your cravat and waistcoat."

He frowned, but slowly loosened the folds of starched linen, then worked free the buttons of the striped silk. The items joined the crumpled coat.

A wave of steel indicated for him to go on. "Your shirt as well."

The earl hesitated. However, after another glance at the pistol clenched in her hand, he undid the fastenings and tugged it over his head.

The flickering candles cast a ripple of light and dark over his muscled shoulders and the chiseled planes of his bare chest. A glint of what might have been grim humor flashed in his amber eyes.

"Do you wish for me to go on?" he asked coolly, his fingers moving to the flap of his breeches. "I am not unused to females seeking out my attention, but this is a rather imaginative approach. Tell me, are you as creative in other techniques as well?"

On seeing his assailant's eyes widen, he gave a curt laugh. "Or perchance have you been sent as some prank by Allenby—though I wouldn't have given him credit for being quite so clever." One button slipped out of its slot. "But whatever your game is, sweeting, don't you think it's time you joined in the spirit of things and removed something as well?

"Hold your tongue!" The sharp order, more shrill than sure, cut off his words. "I'm not interested in any of your lecherous suggestions, sir." The barrel of the gun wavered slightly as her gaze slid along the dusting of dark curls that ran from his breastbone to navel. "I've seen enough. You may put on your clothes—you are not the one."

"How disappointing to hear it. Things were just getting interesting," he murmured softly. "A good deal more interesting than the blasted ledgers with which I was wrestling..."

She ignored the tone of mocking irony. "What other gentlemen are part of this household?"

"What? Having found my flesh wanting, you wish to disrobe

someone else?" The earl's lips curled in a sardonic smile. "With all due modesty, I doubt you will find the footmen—"

"I warn you, do *not* trifle with me!" Her face went rigid with fury as she raised her gaze. "I am quite capable of pulling the trigger, Lord Killingworth. And there is no doubt that you would deserve it just as much as the one I seek."

His eyes narrowed. "Why?" he demanded. He usually had no trouble shrugging off slurs to his character, but somehow her note of scorn struck a raw nerve. "I imagine you do not threaten to put a period to a man's existence without a good reason."

The young lady took a deliberate step forward and aimed the pistol at his heart. But the swagger did not quite reach her eyes. "It is *I* who will ask the questions! Now once again, what other gentlemen are in this house?"

Marcus regarded the weapon calmly. "Surely you do not think a shot will go unnoticed?"

"I have another pistol."

"Ah—but I have considerably more than one servant."

"I shall count to three, sir." Her finger tightened on the trigger. "*One.*"

"If I am to shuffle off this mortal coil, may I at least be permitted to put my shirt back on? I should like to meet my Maker wearing a bit more than when I entered this world." He gave a slight cough. "Besides, I believe you left the window open and it's getting rather chilly in here."

"I imagine it will be a good deal warmer where you are headed," she snapped. However, a curt nod indicated that he might retrieve the cast off garment.

"*Two,*" she added, as he bent to pick it up.

The earl slowly straightened. Suddenly, with a flick of his wrist, the shirt snapped out like a whiplash, knocking the pistol from her hand. Just as quickly, he was at her side, clamping hold of her arm to prevent her from drawing the other weapon.

"Let go of me!" she cried, flailing wildly with her free hand. The fist caught him flush on the mouth, drawing blood.

"Ye gods, you are a real spitfire, aren't you?" he growled, trapping her in a bear hug. In contrast to the hard-edged fury of her limbs, the softness of her tumbled curls was...surprising. As was the subtle sweetness of lavender that scented her skin. It was oddly intriguing that such a fierce creature could possess such beguiling hints of femininity...

An unladylike kick slammed into his shin. Her knee aimed a vicious blow even higher.

"Hell and damnation," Marcus swore, a grimace adding to the lopsided cant of his mouth. He tightened his hold, drawing a grunt of pain. "Enough! Don't force me into doing something we will both regret."

Seeing no chance of freeing herself from his grip, his assailant ceased thrashing. "Go ahead and call the magistrate," she said with a defiant tilt of her chin. "Let them throw me in jail or hang me for this! I shall find some way of seeing justice is done, even if I have to claw my way back from the bowels of Hell to do it."

Marcus could feel the heat of her against his bare skin, but even more searing was the fire in her emerald eyes. Puzzled, he couldn't imagine what had sparked such an intense hostility. No female in her right mind would behave as she had done without good reason —and despite all absence of civilized behavior, she did not appear to be lacking in sanity.

Slowly releasing her, he brushed the back of his hand to his split lip. "Perhaps you would care to explain just what is going on here before any more blood is shed. Mine or yours."

The young lady drew a ragged breath, though in truth she sounded more angry than fearful. "You fine London gentlemen think it a sport to force yourselves on country girls?" she demanded hotly. "And is the game, as you put it, more enjoyable when they are naught but innocents?"

The earl's jaw tightened. "A gentleman does not force himself on *any* female, country or town, innocent or otherwise."

"Ha!" Her look of patent disbelief expressed how much credence she gave to such a statement.

"What makes you think the man you seek is under my roof?" he demanded.

"Given your reputation, Lord Killingworth, it seemed a likely place to start."

"Ah. So, despite my infrequent visits here, I see that I am not unknown in this area."

She crossed her arms and glared at him. "Oh, this may be a small country village but we have all heard the stories about the infamous Black Cat, sir. It is truly an unlucky day for Chertwell that such a mangy feline has chosen to cross our path and take up residence here."

Marcus took a moment to pick up his shirt. "What you just spoke of is not sport, it is a crime. Be assured that no one under this roof is guilty of what you imply," he said quietly. "You have my word on it."

"I have your word on it? How *very* reassuring." Mimicking his earlier mocking tone, the young lady also made an effort to match his cool sneer.

It was a credible job, acknowledged the earl. And to his chagrin, he felt a tinge of color creep to his cheeks. "You have already acknowledged that I am not the responsible party, and there is only my..."

His words pinched off in a frown. "Just how did you decide that I am not the one you seek?" There was another slight pause as he sought a decent way to word his next question. "I take it you, er, saw...a portion of your attacker's anatomy?"

She gripped her arms a bit tighter to her chest. "It wasn't me. It was my..." There was a slight catch in her voice. "My younger sister."

His assailant suddenly appeared a good deal less fierce. She looked away to the fire but the thick fringe of lashes did not quite cover the glitter of tears in her eyes.

"She was returning home from an errand just after dusk when four gentlemen came out of The King's Crown. One offered to escort her home. She declined and he took himself off." There was a harsh intake of breath. "But apparently 'no' is not part of the vocabulary they teach you at Eton and Oxford."

Marcus drew in a harsh breath but refrained from replying.

"Her attacker wore a mask," continued the young woman, her voice barely audible. "But he made no attempt to hide other distinguishing features of his person. His shirt came open in the struggle...baring a distinctive tattoo."

"A *tattoo?*"

"Yes. Of a wolf's head. Indeed, he boasted of how it marked him as a member of a special club—someone who was privileged to live above the rules."

There was silence, save for the crackling of the logs in the hearth.

The earl slipped on his shirt, then walked over to retrieve the fallen pistol. Taking it by the barrel, he weighed it heavily in his hand before returning it to its owner.

"Put this away and go home," he said, suddenly feeling very weary. "I imagine your sister needs you by her side, not on a ship bound for the Antipodes. Or swinging from a gibbet."

She started to protest, but he cut her off.

"What you are looking for now is revenge, not justice. If the guilty party is one of my household, you have my word of honor that he shall answer for his actions."

The young lady stared down at the pistol. It was still primed and cocked, and her finger curled around the trigger

"Don't be a fool," he murmured. "You have shown you possess courage. Show that you have brains to match. Bullets are not the answer. Let me look into the matter. Regardless of what you think of a gentleman's pledge, mine is binding."

There was a reluctant sigh, then the weapon disappeared into her cloak pocket. "I suppose I have little choice tonight but to accede to your wishes." Pulling the cloak tighter around her willowy form, she backed off to the mullioned window and jumped lightly onto the sill. "But don't think that because I am a female, and one without lofty connections, that I can be fobbed off by empty promises for long. If you are lying, I have a pledge of my own—The Black Cat will not have seen the last of me. Or my claws."

With that, she disappeared into the night.

Marcus continued to stare out at his gardens long after the figure had melded into the shadows. Then, swearing softly, he quitted the room, not bothering to gather up the rest of his clothing from the carpet.

* * *

"S-sshir?" The voice was as unsteady as the stumbling steps. "Hope you w'n't waiting up f'r me. Told Ingalls I'd be...late."

Marcus rose from the chair by the bedchamber hearth and regarded the disheveled state of his nephew's dress. The young man's linen was badly rumpled and streaks of mud on his breeches bespoke of several tumbles to the ground.

"Only a fool drinks more than he can hold, Lucien. Haven't I told you that before?"

"I can hold m' liquor." came the defensive mumble. Lucien reached out to steady himself on one of the carved bedposts and nearly missed catching hold of it. "No more foxed than t'others. Jez tired, izz all."

The earl's mouth tightened, but he willingly changed the subject. "Who were you with?"

"Stonef'rth. Barr'nton." The young man winced slightly from the effort of trying to force his thoughts into coherent order. "Oh, and D'Quincy." His hand raked through his tangled locks. "Where the devil izz Ingalls with m'dressing gown? Need t' lie down."

"You may do so after we have finished our little talk," replied Marcus.

Lucien's head snapped up at the sharpness of the earl's voice.

"You were at The King's Crown?" he went on.

"Y-yes, sir." The words sounded a trifle less slurred.

"Doing what?"

"E-enjoying a few pints. And a bottle or two of b-brandy, I s'pose." Lucien swallowed hard. "Mayhap a hand of cards as well."

Marcus leaned against the mantel. "So, rather the same as you have been doing for every night this past week."

A flush stole to the young man's cheeks. "Sir, if Barrington haz suggested I can't cover m' vowels, I beg t'assure you my losses weren't so—"

"Was wenching a part of the evenings as well?" interrupted Marcus.

Lucien's color deepened. "I—I'm as game as any m-man f'r a grope and a poke," he muttered, avoiding the earl's gaze.

"No doubt," replied Marcus, keeping his voice neutral. "Any of the barmaids or local farm girls catch your fancy? There are a number of comely lasses in the area, are there not?"

Lucien looked puzzled by all the questions, and by the earl's seemingly erratic mood. "I—that is, there's one girl. A pretty blond who I've noticed s'veral times before. I walked with her f'r a bit."

"Did you tumble her?"

"What's t' fuss if I did or not?" mumbled Lucien, rubbing at his temples in some confusion. "It's been deucedly boring rusticating here in the country. Surely you aren't going to kick up a dust over havin' a bit of f-fun. Why, the stories of *your* carousing in Town are legend—

"It is not *my* behavior we are discussing here, it is yours." The earl took a step closer to his nephew. "I asked you a question, Lucien. I expect an answer.

"I...I might have. I—I don't remember," came the sullen reply.

"You don't remember," repeated Marcus softly. "You force yourself on some female and *You. Don't. Remember*?"

"How can I be expected to remember? I was in my cups—"

Before Lucien could finish his excuse, the earl hit him, a bruising blow that knocked him flat to the carpet.

Dazed, the young man struggled to sit up. His nose was bloodied and his cheek turning an ugly shade of purple. "I d-don't understand! What have I done?" he groaned.

"A despicable act. And one not befitting of anyone who dares call himself a gentleman. You miserable cur. Get up!"

The earl reached down and hauled his nephew to his feet. Although the young man was nearly as tall as he was, Marcus shook him like a terrier would a rat. "You will present yourself in the breakfast room at nine o'clock this morning." Shoving Lucien onto the bed with a grimace of disgust, he turned for the door. "And I shall expect you to be dressed for an important occasion."

"W-what occasion, sir?" stammered his nephew.

The earl's smile was frightening in its coldness. "Oh, as to that, you will learn it soon enough."

"Hmmmph."

Eliza Kirtland penned in the last set of the figures and tallied the sums. After checking over the pages one last time, she shut the account book with a satisfying snap and stacked it atop the others on her desk.

Now that she had marshaled her proof, the numbers arranged in precise columns like the crème de la crème of Wellington's troops, Squire Newton would have to be daft not to surrender to her suggestions. Still, the fellow was wont to be extremely pig-headed about such things, even though her advice had proven useful over the last few years.

And yet the phalanx of figures was unassailable. By switching from rye to barley, and by utilizing the newest theory of crop rotation—as well as by cutting back on cows and adding more sheep—his income should double over the next six months.

A wry sigh slipped from Eliza's lips. Of course, there would be the usual dire mutterings about the risk of changing from age-old traditions. A glass of sherry would be downed, followed quickly by a second one. Then, after another round of grousing on how females did not understand the nuances of either business or farming, the squire would grudgingly agree to put her suggestions into practice.

She wouldn't even have to muster much of an argument. The numbers spoke for themselves. And the prospect of a full purse was more convincing than any words she might utter.

Eliza looked back to the pile of ledgers. The squire wasn't the only local to have profited from her cleverness with figures. Even as a young girl she had possessed a head for numbers and a penchant for practicality—attributes that had allowed her family to live in a good deal more comfort than her father's meager income should have allowed. After noting her deft handling of the church fund for the poor, the local butcher had requested her help in balancing his books.

Word soon spread concerning her knack for maximizing returns while cutting expenses, and she soon had a thriving little business in handling accounts. Nowadays, more than a few of the local gentry and merchants depended on her skill and savvy in helping to oversee their endeavors.

Her talents made it possible for her family to continue living in the manner to which they had become accustomed, despite the death of her father. And though her mother fretted that her oldest daughter was forced to earn a living for them all, Eliza didn't mind in the least. She enjoyed being useful.

Useful.

Eliza tapped the tip of the pen to her chin. *Was that how most people viewed her?*

A sigh. Well, she hadn't been very useful last night. Lud, what had possessed her to burst into a gentleman's house and threaten him with a pistol? It was most unlike her to act in such a wild, impulsive manner, letting heated emotion override common sense.

And much good it had done her.

Her fingers tightened as she recalled how easily the Earl of Killingworth had overpowered her. It had taken barely a flick of his muscled arm, and suddenly the steely strength of his fingers had trapped her inexorably within his grasp.

The very memory of his touch sent a strange frisson of fire along her spine. She was surprised the imprint of those lithe fingers wasn't singed onto her skin, so aware had she been of their heat. Just as from the moment he had looked up at her with those hooded amber eyes, she had been acutely aware of his rampant masculinity. Even clothed, he had radiated a raw animal magnetism. But when he had removed his shirt, the sight of such naked, chiseled power had ignited an inexplicable response.

It was simply a burning contempt, she assured herself, and not any other reaction. It had nothing to do with the fact that being pressed up against the hard length of his body had been oddly comforting. Or that, for an instant, a flicker in those luminous eyes had hinted at a sympathy she wouldn't have imagined possible in a rakish scoundrel...

Eliza stared in mute consternation at the snapped pen in her hands and felt a heat seep up to her cheeks. Muttering a word that no rector's daughter should have known, she hid the two pieces in her desk drawer. If only she might shove such disturbing thoughts back into the darkest recesses of her mind as well. It was a measure of how overset her nerves had become that she would, even for an instant, imagine that a man like Killingworth might offer some measure of support.

Even more ridiculous was the notion that she might have need of anyone to lean on, especially a dissolute rakehell. She was too busy being a pillar of strength for everyone around her.

And as for the strange flames licking up inside her—well, that was simply the conflagration of worry and anger. And perhaps a spark of surprise. The earl had not been at all what she had expected.

Her lips quirked. Not that she had any idea of how a jaded London rake and notorious libertine ought to appear. However, she supposed she had imagined someone more...debauched looking. Someone whose fuzzed features and clammy touch would betray his dissolute dedication to wanton habits. Instead, the flickering candlelight had limned an austere, aristocratic face, forbidding in its chiseled contours.

A small swallow caught in her throat. *Forbidden.* Mayhap that was more the word. She felt hot...and then cold. He was all the things she loathed in a man—sinfully handsome, supremely selfish, overbearingly high-handed. Surely she could not be attracted to anyone like that.

"Loathsome, *loathsome* man," she whispered, hoping the harsh sound would serve to reinforce such sentiment. Even though it appeared he was not guilty of the crime in question, there was little doubt that he embodied exactly the sort of condescending pride she found so abhorrent in the opposite sex. It was there in the arrogant tilt of his lean jaw, the sardonic twist of his sensuous lips and the raking gaze of his amber eyes. Eyes made even more imperious by the dark arch of his brows.

No matter that he spoke of honor. *Ha!* If the rumors had only a grain of truth to them, such words lilting off his tongue made a mockery of the notion. To hear his tenants repeat the stories that had drifted down from London, the lord of the manor cared for naught but the pursuit of pleasure. Drinking, wagering, seducing a goodly number of other men's wives—there appeared to be few, if any, vices the Earl of Killingworth was not intimately acquainted with.

But honor?

A host of adjectives might be used to describe the earl, but 'honorable' was not among the first that came to mind. Eliza doubted the concept meant anything more to him than the fact that he must not shirk from covering his gaming vowels or meeting a disgruntled husband's dawn challenge on Hounslow Heath.

After a moment's consideration, her lips slowly curved in disdain as she added another word to the list.

Foolish.

Besides being an indolent wastrel, the earl must be a hopeless fool to boot. For only someone devoid of all common sense would let such a magnificent estate as Killingworth Manor fall into such a state of neglect. Why, the rich fields and lush pasturelands should be yielding a handsome return, but from what she had heard, the place was running at a considerable loss.

Her fingers drummed on her desk. And he was an even bigger fool if he thought idle promises would put her off for long.

As if in answer to the agitated tattoo, a large marmalade cat jumped down from the window still, purring loudly as it settled itself in her lap.

Eliza smiled as a paw batted at an errant curl that had come loose from its pins. "Well, Caliban, I may have been no more effective than an old tabby last night, but His Lordship has better take note that my claws will not remain sheathed for long."

* * *

"*WHAT!*" LUCIEN'S FACE WENT EVEN PALER, accentuating the heavy mottling on his cheek and the dark smudges under his eyes.

Marcus didn't look up from his newspaper. The freshly ironed page turned with a snap as he took a sip of his coffee.

"Lord Almighty! You can't mean it!" added his nephew in a horrified whisper.

"Can't I?" Another page rustled. "You must still be a trifle bosky if you are confusing me with the Deity on High." The earl put down his cup. "With Him you might pray for forgiveness, but with me you are wasting your breath. I will tolerate many things, but never a breach of honor. You knew the rules. If you were in the throes of carnal lust, you should have chosen an experienced woman—or paid one."

"But sir!" The note of panic in Lucien's voice rose as he pressed his palms to his brow. "M-m-marriage? Why, I've only spoken to the girl a couple of times. I have no real acquaintance with her," he stammered.

"You should have thought of that before you forced an innocent—no matter what her position in Society—to toss up her skirts."

"I...I didn't mean to! Indeed, I have no recollection of it at all —" He broke off and took a deep breath.

"Which is precisely why I advised you in the past not to imbibe more than you could tolerate without losing control of your senses."

Lucien suddenly looked up with a glimmer of hope. "How are you so sure it was me? I mean, the others were as drunk as I was."

"Do you know anyone else in this area who sports the tattoo of a wolf's head on his breast?"

The young man bit at his lip.

"I also warned you that joining such a club was not wise."

His nephew fisted his hands. "It's not fair!" he blurted out.

"I am no more pleased than you are that your parents saw fit to name me as your guardian. They never informed me of the arrangement. But as you don't come of age for another year, you are still my ward."

"Nine months, twelve days to be exact." Lucien kicked at the carpet. "You cannot force me into marriage," he muttered.

"No, I cannot," agreed Marcus with a grim smile. "As I said, the choice is yours. You can marry the girl. Or you can accompany me to the magistrate, where I shall be forced to press charges against you for assault and rape." He paused to butter a slice of toast. "Because of your age and rank, you might only be transported, rather than hanged."

His nephew gave a convulsive swallow.

"Now then, have you made up your mind?"

Lucien's voice was hardly more than a hoarse croak. "I'll m-m-marry her."

"I rather thought you might." The earl finally looked up. "Do you, perchance, know her name?"

"Mari—no...Meredith."

"Family name?"

His nephew was silent for a moment. "I'm not sure. I think it may be Kirtland."

"Any idea as to where she lives, or what her family does?"

Lucien shook his head.

The earl turned attention back to the newspaper. "Well, we should be able to discover the information soon enough with a few discreet inquiries in town." He rang for a fresh pot of coffee. "I suggest you have something to eat before we leave. I imagine it will be a rather long and trying day."

His nephew made a choking sound, and looked as if he might be sick. Then, casting a look of pure venom at the earl, he rose and fled from the room.

Marcus let out a harried sigh as the door slammed shut. Pushing aside his toast, he turned to stare out the window, anger and dismay leaving a bitter taste in his mouth.

Bloody hell, what had his sister been thinking? She and her husband must have had windmills in their heads to imagine he was the proper sort of guardian for anyone. Why, he had only met his nephew a handful of times before the influenza epidemic had turned him into a surrogate parent. Even then, the lad had quickly been packed off to Eton. Between holidays spent with school friends and his own frequent travels, contact between them had hardly been more frequent.

It was only several weeks ago, when Lucien had finished his studies at Oxford, that the earl's man of affairs had strongly advised that the young man be summoned to Killingworth Manor. Duty demanded a discussion regarding Lucien's plans for the future—at least until he came into his majority, and with it the tidy inheritance left by his father. The earl had grudgingly yielded to the suggestion, though the last thing he desired was a visit from an utter stranger.

Especially as the estate required his full attention.

Marcus grimaced at the irony of the situation. Here he was, lamenting the twist of fate that had made him responsible for someone he hardly knew. And yet, he was about to force the same fate upon his nephew, not for a paltry few years, but for life. The young man could hardly be blamed for looking as though he, too, would like to take dead aim with a pistol at the earl's heart.

In truth, Lucien had more than a little of his sympathy, despite his outward show of callous indifference. However, he could see no way out of the coil. Contrary to the rumors regarding his own rakish reputation, Marcus had never tolerated dishonorable behavior, either in himself or others. He simply couldn't turn his head at this egregious crime.

Not even for his sister's son.

Lucien knew the rules governing a gentleman's behavior. And yet, he had chosen to break one of the most basic tenets. The consequences had been spelled out in just as much detail. No matter how harsh the punishment seemed in retrospect, it must be accepted.

Marcus found his thoughts drifting to the bizarre scene of last night, and the cloaked figure who had sought to mete out her own justice. *Right and wrong.* He wished he knew just what sort of man his nephew really was. Lucien seemed remorseful, but did he merely regret being caught? Had the act been an unfortunate aberration in character? Or was the young man a depraved creature capable of casual cruelty without a thought for aught but his own selfish desires?

With a twinge of guilt, the earl realized that he really hadn't a clue. As an oath slipped from his lips, he found himself adding a silent prayer that Lucien wouldn't prove to be an utter scoundrel.

His decision was affecting not only his nephew's fate, but also the lives of others.

Pushing away from the table, his coffee as cold as his hopes, Marcus reluctantly quitted the comfort of his breakfast room.

Duty, however onerous, could not be denied.

Three

Lucien's expression was more befitting a funeral than a wedding. He threw himself against the carriage squabs and turned to stare out the window. His hand rubbed his cheek, as if it might be possible to banish the bruise, along with the other ghastly consequences of his carousing.

Marcus took a seat beside his nephew and called for the horses to be sprung. Ignoring the young man's sullen silence, he fell to studying the papers in his lap. It was of some benefit to have competent servants, he thought with a grim smile. As well as a lofty title and an adequate purse. His valet had managed the purchase of a special license, while the head footman had learned enough from the innkeeper to avoid embarrassing public inquiries as to where the young lady lived.

His lips thinned on regarding the last fact. It appeared that the situation was even messier than he had imagined. The injured party was the daughter of a rector. With a harried sigh, he crumpled the sheet and shoved it in his pocket, restraining the urge to take his nephew by the collar and give him yet another shake.

A quarter mile past the village of Chertwell, the carriage turned onto a narrow lane lined with high hedgerows. It passed several small farms before stopping before a large cottage whose whitewashed walls were like a splash of fresh cream against the dappled greens of the surrounding fields. The dwelling was set off from the road by a low stone wall, heavy with honeysuckle. Its sweet perfume scented the morning breeze.

Marcus had to nudge his nephew twice before the young man managed to rise from his seat.

A profusion of daffodils bordered the pebbled path that lead to the front door. Despite its obvious age, the cottage looked to be a cozy place, with trellised roses climbing up its weathered sides and a hint of cheerful chintz behind the spotless leaded windows.

The earl took his place by Lucien's side, pausing for a moment to smooth a crease from his coat. "Head up, shoulders square," he growled. "I expect you to comport yourself with at least an outward show of dignity, as befits a gentleman." There was a slight pause. "Though in truth I'm not sure you deserve the title."

Lucien swallowed hard, shooting the earl a look that mingled equal parts resentment and fear. Despite such emotions, his chin came up and he managed a firm stride. They mounted the steps together, but there his courage seemed to flag.

It was Marcus who reached up and rapped the iron knocker.

There was no answer.

"P-Perhaps we should come back at a later time," mumbled the young man, not daring to look over at the earl's rigid face.

Marcus knocked again, this time with more force.

The door came slightly ajar. After a slight hesitation, he pushed it open. There was still no sign of anyone.

"Uncle Marcus—"

The earl silenced him with a brusque wave and stepped into the entrance foyer. He took in the plain appointments, then slowly moved into a narrow passageway, motioning Lucien to follow. It gave entrance to a sunny little parlor, bright with scrubbed pine and faded chintz florals. A large desk, its surface nearly obscured by books and papers, dominated the space near the windows. Atop the stack, Marcus caught sight of several of the latest new manuals on agriculture.

Restraining the urge to have a closer look, he forced his gaze to move on. At the far end of the room, a door was open to the sunlight. It revealed a large garden, whose original shape had long since grown into a delightful twist of nooks and crannies, now filled with flowers and herbs.

Marcus finished his cursory survey. Satisfied that no one was around, he was ready to retrace his steps when a young lady suddenly appeared from outdoors, cradling a basket of cut greens. Head bent, she was halfway across the room before she noticed the two gentlemen.

Her gasp was punctuated by the crack of woven willow hitting the floor.

"Forgive us if we have startled you," said the earl. "I assure you, there is no reason to be alarmed."

There could be little doubt as to her identity. As the innkeeper had described, Meredith Kirtland was a very pretty girl, with guinea-gold hair, azure eyes and rosebud lips that had likely inspired more than one young man to try his hand at poetry.

At the moment, however, Marcus saw that those lovely features were shaded in fear. With good reason—her cheek had been bruised by a hard blow, and several deep scratches cut across her neck.

"Is your father at home?" he added quietly. "I wish to speak with—"

A rustling of skirts in the hallway caused Marcus to break off his question.

"Merry, have you fetched the chamomile and—"

The voice was all too familiar. As were the clenched fists and flashing green eyes.

"Get out!" His erstwhile assailant shoved past him and took up a stance to shield her sister. "At once!"

The halo of unruly blonde curls—a deeper, redder shade than that of her sibling—put the earl in mind of an ancient Valkyrie. All that was missing was a sword.

Her tongue, however, was just as cutting. "How dare you despicable men force your way into our home!"

The earl's jaw tightened. Her verbal attack was threatening to turn an awkward confrontation into a full-scale battle. Reminding himself that she had good reason to be upset, he answered with what he thought was a show of great patience. "I did knock. But as no one appeared, and the door was half open, I took it upon myself to enter. I think you might agree that the circumstances merit a certain urgency."

The appeal to reason only sparked a scowl.

"I had hoped to find your father present..." He let his words trail off in question.

This time the young lady obliged him with an answer. "My father has been dead for two years, sir."

Marcus cleared his throat. "A brother, perhaps?"

"If you are casting about for the head of the family, you have found her," she snapped. "My mother has been in ill health for some time, and this morning she was stricken with another bout of chest pains. That is why both the housekeeper and I were upstairs and did not hear a knock."

Exhaling a ragged breath, she added softly, "Any knowledge of what has happened would likely kill her outright."

After a tiny pause, her voice once again hardened to a sharp edge. "What is it you want? Why are you here? I cannot imagine why you would think that anyone in this family would care to set eyes on either of you scoundrels."

It was not as if he expected a cordial greeting. But neither had he anticipated such a scathing assault on his character. The vengeful Valkyrie was not even allowing him the chance to explain himself. Angry with his nephew for putting him in such a damnably awkward position—and with the lady for being so rigidly righteous, Marcus felt his own temper growing dangerously frayed.

Somehow he managed to keep his voice even. "I made a promise to look into the matter, and as I told you, my word—however worthless you consider it—is binding. It appears you were correct in thinking your sister's assailant was a member of my household." He took Lucien by the arm and forced him forward. "My nephew is here to—"

The young lady, on the other hand, made no effort to disguise her fury. Yet again, a violent outburst interrupted his explanation. "You presume to bring that mongrel, that *beast*, anywhere near my sister?" She pointed at Lucien, who flinched as though he had been skewered with steel. "After what he has done!"

"I-I..." Lucien tried to speak but all that came out was a croak.

"He is extremely sorry for what happened," intervened the earl. "Apparently he had consumed a great deal of spirits and was lost to all sense of reason." The young lady was making it extremely difficult to maintain a measured tone.

Bloody hell, did she think he was any more pleased with the situation than she was?

"That, of course, is no excuse for his actions," he went on. "But he is prepared to do the honorable thing and make amends for his conduct. I have procured a special license. Your sister may be properly wed before nightfall."

The young lady stared with withering scorn at the document, then slowly raised her eyes to meet his. "Are you *mad*? Do you really think my sister would consider for an instant legshackling herself to such a filthy miscreant as your nephew?"

She turned back to Lucien, a sneer thinning her mouth as she eyed his bruises. "Honorable, you say? Oh, yes, I can see just how eager he was to do the honorable thing." Her hands clenched. "Perhaps you, too, are completely jug bitten. I can't think of how else to explain why you might imagine such an offer would be of any interest to us."

"You are overset at this moment," began Marcus.

"Overset?" she repeated with marked sarcasm. "My sister has just been cruelly assaulted! Overset doesn't *begin* to describe what I am feeling at this moment."

Gritting his teeth, Marcus managed to ignore the repeated insults, though the effort was costing him dearly. "I would counsel you to think long and hard before rejecting the proposal. My nephew is from an excellent family, and as of now, he stands heir to an earldom. Not only that, he shall come into a tidy inheritance of his own on reaching his majority. A great many Mamas of the *ton* would consider him an excellent catch." He darted a pointed look at the modest furnishings. "All in all, I don't imagine that a country rector's daughter could hope to look any higher."

"Higher?" scoffed the young lady. "As far as I can see, we would have to dig in the deepest, foulest muck to find a creature as loathsome as your slimy relative." She gave a protective squeeze to her sister's shoulder, who had finally summoned enough courage to raise her gaze from the floor.

Hell and damnation. Muttering an oath under his breath, Marcus could not refrain from taking the offensive. "Have you given any thought to the possible consequences?" he said harshly. "Your sister may find herself with..."

The girl flinched.

He stopped abruptly, angry with himself for allowing his antagonist to goad him into such bluntness. Despite what she seemed to think, the last thing he wished to do was add to her sister's suffering.

"Forgive me. I suggest that we continue this discussion in private, Miss..."

"Kirtland." The young lady finally consented to confirm her identity. "Elizabeth Kirtland."

"I fear there is no way to avoid plain speaking. And such things will no doubt prove too upsetting for your sister's ears."

Eliza hesitated, then gave a curt nod. "Mama is waiting for her tisane, Merry. Might you manage to take it up to her by yourself?"

Meredith Kirtland spoke for the first time, softly but firmly. "Nay, Eliza. I understand your concern, but it is my wish—and indeed my right—to stay and hear what is being said."

Eliza looked torn between the sense of her sister's words and the desire to shield her from more pain. It took another whispered exchange before she relented. With a brusque wave of her hand, she signaled for Marcus to continue.

He waited for a moment to see if she might change her mind "Very well, then. As I was saying, before you reject the offer out of hand, have you considered that your sister may find herself with child? Even if she does not, her future prospects of marriage have no doubt been greatly compromised, if not ruined outright."

The elder Kirtland sister fixed both him and Lucien with a look of contempt. "Our local midwife has examined her. Judging from that, and what my sister was able to recount, it seems your nephew did not actually..." A tinge of color rose to her cheeks. "That is, my sister was pawed over and vilely humiliated in the most intimate of ways, but there was no actual...consummation of the act." Her eyes pressed shut for an instant. "I suppose we must be grateful for small favors."

Lucien's face went from deathly pale to a vivid scarlet as he gave a convulsive swallow.

Recovering her composure, Eliza went on. "And any man who truly cares for Meredith will not hold her to blame for being pawed over against her will."

The earl made no effort to hide the cynical curl of his lips. "You have a more sanguine view of human nature than I would have expected. Let me assure you that men can be quite unreasonable about that sort of thing." He saw a flicker of doubt cross her face. "Once your anger has cooled, I urge you to think over my nephew's offer very carefully."

There was an awkward silence as their gazes locked. *Steel against steel.* Marcus was surprised the clash of metal was not ringing in his ears.

He slowly withdrew a purse from his pocket. He placed it on the side table, next to a basket of sewing. "In the meantime, if your sister has need of anything, this may serve to help. And if you are truly bent on rejecting the offer of marriage, I should be willing to arrange for a suitable dowry, one that might help smooth things with any future suitor."

However reasonable they sounded to him, his words seemed only to rekindle the fire in Eliza's eyes.

"Take your filthy purse and be gone, sir! In London, your money may be adequate recompense for the pleasures you take, but not here."

So much for thinking that logic might prevail.

"No doubt you look at us poor country folk as mere chattel to be used as you please. Well, no amount of coins will ever pay for what you have done to my sister, you debauched wastrel."

The earl stiffened. If she were a man, he would not hesitate to demand satisfaction for the slur. *A duel at dawn?* That, of course, was out of the question. Or was it? With a flash of grim humor, he recalled her obvious experience with wielding a weapon. Why, if looks could kill, those molten emerald eyes—

Just how he had come to be thinking of their intriguing color took him aback for an instant. He shook away such distracting thoughts and quickly parried her cut with a thrust of his own.

"You deliberately misinterpret my words, Miss Kirtland. If you would temper your anger with a modicum of reason, you would see your accusations are unjust. My nephew has offered marriage. If that is not acceptable, I am simply trying to find some other way to offer amends for the damage that has been done."

"Nothing can make amends for that!"

He met her fiery words with an icy stare. "Then what is it you would like?"

Eliza pointed at Lucien. "To see him suffer! To see him transported or swinging from the gibbet for what he has done."

"No, I cannot allow that." Marcus's jaw set in an intractable line. "Lucien is willing to abide by what honor demands and give your sister the protection of his name. I will not ask more than that from him."

"I could press charges."

"Don't be a fool," he snapped. "We both know it would only further harm your sister." His eyes avoided Meredith. "No magistrate would act on such a charge. My nephew could always claim that she was...willing. Do you doubt that his word would be accepted over hers?"

"I—"

Meredith laid a hand on Eliza's arm. "I know you mean well, but I do not wish to argue anymore. Lord Killingworth and his nephew have offered to take responsibility for what has happened. It is, I imagine, a generous offer. Though not one we wish to accept. The matter is finished."

"But—"

"Let it go, Eliza. It is what I wish."

The trill notes of a robin's song wafted from the garden, an incongruous counterpoint to the harsh words still echoing in the grim silence.

"Very well. If that is what you wish." Eliza looked away. "Good day, gentlemen."

Lucien fell back a step, but then hesitated, hands clenched tightly at his side. "I...didn't mean to hurt you," he stammered. "Never have I done such a..." Words seemed to elude him. "I—I am so very sorry."

The earl rather expected another round of invectives, but as Eliza turned and met the haunted look in his nephew's eyes, she heaved a sigh. "Aren't we all?"

It was impossible to make out Meredith's expression for she had retreated into the flickering shadows.

He took hold of Lucien's sleeve and started him toward the door. "You know where to find us if you have a change of mind." He left the purse where it lay.

"Oh yes, I certainly do, Lord Killingworth." Eliza spoke just loudly enough for him to hear her parting shot.

"But Hell is where the likes of you and your nephew belong."

Four

Meredith knelt down and began to gather up the herbs from the floor. "I had better start on Mama's tisane," she said softly, her features still hidden from any scrutiny. Without waiting for a response, she took up her basket and hurried toward the kitchen.

It took a moment for Eliza to realize that her hands were so tightly clenched that her nails had drawn blood. Looking down, she quirked a rueful grimace and forced herself to relax. It would seem that the term "seeing red" was not merely an old wives' expression for a fit of blinding anger. Such a display of raw emotion left her feeling both stunned and a little shaken.

Strong, steady, unbending. A female with deeply rooted notions of principles and purpose. And one as unlikely to snap in the face of a storm as the towering oak behind the village tavern.

Now *that* was the Eliza Kirtland most people would recognize, including herself. Though, to be honest, there were others—people to whom she had stood up to over the years—who would no doubt use less flattering adjectives. Stubborn and strong-willed were among the first to come to mind.

Well, whatever the nuance of language, something had broken

her self-control as if it were naught but a twig. The crime against her sister had been a monstrous one, to be sure, but was it that alone which had sparked such passion? For along with anger and a desire for revenge was another powerful emotion she couldn't put a name to.

Or didn't dare to.

Her nails nearly dug fresh furrows in her palms. The brutal truth was, her heart had nearly skipped a beat on seeing the Earl of Killingworth in the doorway of the parlor. In daylight, his shoulders looked even more sculpted, his height even more imposing, his profile even more handsome...

No! It simply could not be possible that she felt any attraction to one of the most notorious libertines in the land. Much less one that was so intensely...physical.

Even in her youth she had never been foolish enough to fall into girlish raptures over an attractive face or casual compliment. So surely she was not now, at such an advanced age, succumbing to sheer lunacy.

And yet it was hard to deny that he aroused feelings that defied mere words.

A shiver shuddered through her.

She took a deep breath. It was not as if she disliked men in general. Not really. There were several of her acquaintances who merited her regard. However, the trouble was that most of them seemed lacking in any of the qualities that engendered real respect. And those shortcomings were only exacerbated by the fact that they were accorded authority by virtue of their plumbing rather than their brains.

The utter unfairness of it elicited another grimace. One had only to look at the earl to realize the justness of her anger. By all accounts Killingworth was naught but a drunkard and rake. Talk of his outrageous luck at the gaming tables had reached even so small a village as Chertwell. As had word of his prowess in the boudoirs of Town. And yet, he was the one who had the power to decide what justice was. Why, with no more than a curt word, he could affect the course of their lives and—

Eliza stopped herself from such pointless railing. There would be time enough later to dwell on the shortcomings of the earl and his ilk. Right now she had best go in to her sister.

Meredith was bent over a large iron kettle. "Are they gone?" she asked softly as she stirred a mixture of chopped herbs into the boiling water.

"Yes." Eliza brushed a lock of a hair from her sister's cheek. "And I doubt very much whether they shall return."

Meredith essayed a smile. "You certainly raked His Lordship over the coals. Though I'm not sure it was quite wise to risk igniting his ire. After all, since he owns the living to the parish, he does have the power to turn us out from this cottage if he so chooses."

"Let him try," she muttered.

Another handful of greens went into the brew. "You needn't be so worried about me, you know. I am not quite so fragile as you think." Meredith added a crumble of willow bark. "I—I imagine it will take some time before the nightmares fade, or before I can see a man approach without flinching. But I shall get over it." She forced her chin up. "Something of value may have been stolen from me, but I shall not let anyone take away what is really impor-tant—my self-respect."

Eliza's voice caught in her throat. "I shall take care never to underestimate you again, Merry. Thank heaven that your special gift for healing people extends to yourself as well." She shook her head. "How is it that you are so wise beyond your years?"

"Perhaps because I have been listening to you for so long."

They exchanged fierce hugs, then Meredith dabbed at her eyes with the sleeve of her gown. "Let us bring Mama her tisane."

"I'll do it, if you would rather lie down." Eliza touched her sister's swollen eye.

"I—I would rather keep busy. And you needn't worry that

Mama is going to be upset by my appearance. I already told her that I fell along the riverbank while foraging for cress."

"Brave girl," murmured Eliza. "Come then, we'll go together"

* * *

"WELL, IT APPEARS YOU HAVE MORE LUCK THAN YOU deserve." The earl waved a brusque signal to his coachman. "You may escape this sordid business without any consequences. Though I warn you, the lady may well change her mind on thinking the matter over. If she does, I shall still expect you to do your duty."

He clamped his high crowned beaver hat back on his head. "In the future," he added harshly, "I shall also expect you to control your drinking and to sheath your sword in naught but willing scabbards. If anything like this happens again, I'll see you shipped off to some godforsaken plantation in Jamaica, do you understand me?"

Lucien's only reply was a stifled groan as he grabbed for the carriage door. His fingers slipped on the latch and he fell heavily against the lacquered wood. "Sweet Jesus," he groaned. "Did you see that poor girl's face? And the way she looked at me as if I were some sort of depraved...monster?" His fist hit the paneling. "I can't believe I could ever have done such a horrible thing to another person. I—"

A violent retching cut off his words. It was several moments before the young man managed to gain control of his heaving stomach.

Repressing a harried sigh, Marcus took a handkerchief from his pocket and thrust it into Lucien's hand before helping him into the carriage. Once inside, his nephew turned away and slumped back against the squabs, eyes closed, the silk square pressed to his lips.

The earl was not unhappy with the prospect of silence for the journey home. He, too, shifted to face the glass, but the fields of spring wheat and flocks of sheep passed by in a blur.

Hell's teeth. Things had gone much worse than he had imagined—as if that was possible.

He massaged at his brow. Given the circumstances, what, exactly, had he expected? Anger, certainly, and hurt. That was only natural. But he had also thought to see just a glimmer of gratitude as well, for the willingness to offer a country girl of modest means something that few gentlemen would have felt obliged to give.

Gratitude? Ha! There had been nothing but scorn and loathing in Miss Eliza Kirtland's flashing green eyes. It was hard to blame her, of course. The deed had been a dastardly one, and she looked rather young to be bearing sole responsibility for her family. And it didn't help matters that gossip about his own past apparently had as little trouble circulating through the countryside of Devonshire as it did through the drawing rooms of Mayfair.

Still, he had made every attempt to act honorably and it piqued him that she had dismissed his efforts so out of hand.

The devil take it. She was certainly unlike any other female of his acquaintance. The sharpness of her claws and the fierceness of her words reminded him once again of a tiger. Why, even her hair had a hint of russet highlights.

She had a tiger's courage as well, he admitted grudgingly, to go along with her protective instincts. How many young ladies would dare to march into a titled lord's library brandishing pistols? Not to speak of hurling such deliberate insults in his face. He rubbed at his jaw. And how many females would be so stubbornly principled as to reject the offer of status and a tidy fortune?

Yes, the snappish, snarling Miss Kirtland was indeed unique.

Would that she remained so, and didn't change her mind about this blasted mess. He would be as pleased as the young lady if their paths never crossed again. The last thing he needed at the moment—besides a troublesome ward—was a troublesome female in his life. He had more than enough difficulties to cope with as it was.

Yet some odd stirring of his body refused to acknowledge the admonitions of his brain.

Distracting himself from such disturbing thoughts, Marcus slanted a quick glance at Lucien. His anger had slowly been replaced by exasperation, and even a touch of sympathy. Perhaps he deserved some of the blame for what had happened. It could not have been easy for the young man to lose loving parents at a tender age, only to find them replaced by an aloof guardian. One who, admittedly, showed little interest in his very existence, much less his wellbeing.

Damnation. The earl acknowledged his own shortcomings with a silent oath. He should have made more of an effort to get to know his ward and offer some counsel. After all, Lucien was his heir, and that alone should have demanded that he pay some attention to the young man's development.

His lips compressed in a tight line. At least it appeared that his nephew was not a hardened scoundrel, despite the lack of any fatherly guidance. That the girl's condition had elicited such gut-wrenching remorse only confirmed that Lucien did indeed possess a conscience. And a rather tender one at that.

The earl found himself chalking it up as a large mark in the young man's favor. Now, he supposed it was up to him to try to discover what other qualities—good or bad—Lucien possessed.

But had the breach of disinterest and distrust between them become so gaping that it would be impossible to bridge?

Marcus's brooding gaze followed the bumps and jags of the weathered stone fence that bordered the road. He could not help but wonder whether his harsh reaction had as much to do with his own past transgressions as those of his nephew. Perhaps the young man was an uncomfortable reminder of himself, and things he would much rather not be forced to remember.

Drinking, seduction, deep play at cards. It had all been a game for him and his friends, seeing just how close to the edge they could push one another without falling into the chasm. He had been very, very good at it. More times than he cared to remember, he had drunk far more than Lucien ever had. Oh, he had never committed so blatant an offence as forcing his attentions on an innocent young lady. Even in his deepest cups, he had known not to break certain rules. He had simply mastered the art of bending them to his own purpose.

There had seemed little harm in it. After all, it was only a game.

Indeed, his friends, and the majority of the *ton*, had looked at him with something akin to awe for such ability. His exploits were legendary—in the gambling hells, in the daredevil escapades, and most especially in the boudoirs. Dubbed 'The Black Cat' for his sinuous skill in nocturnal prowlings, the moniker had stuck. Not only did he seem to bring bad luck to anyone who dared challenge him, but his penchant for escaping unscathed from tight spots made it appear that he possessed nine lives.

For a brief moment, Marcus's hand strayed over his eyes, as if it could block out the disquieting memories.

Perhaps if he had been able to pass on one of those lives to Fitzwilliam Burnley he wouldn't find sleep so damn elusive at night. Most everyone held him blameless for what happened. A curricle race carried with it the risk of a crash. If the burden of guilt was to rest anywhere, it was squarely on the shoulders of anyone reckless enough to climb onto the perch.

Marcus knew better. He should never have baited his friend into attempting the dangerous drive. Fitz was cow-handed to begin with, and after several bottles of brandy he had no business taking hold of the ribbons...

The carriage finally passed through the iron gates and made the last turn to the stately manor house. As the earl stared at the towering elms lining the way, he felt his spirits lift somewhat. The ever-resilient cycle of nature never ceased to amaze him. It seemed so impossible that bare sticks could withstand the harsh elements and then spring to life at the first touch of warmth. Perhaps that was also why he found some measure of solace in his estate. With crops and livestock it was the same sort of satisfaction—one could see tangible results from hard work and careful nurturing.

Next to him, Lucien stirred in his seat, the play of shadows throwing a pattern of light and dark across his mottled cheek. The earl repressed a harried sigh, wishing the intricacies of people—and the human heart—were half so easy to figure out.

As the horses came to a halt, his nephew grabbed for the door latch, obviously eager to make his escape.

"A moment, Lucien."

"Sir?" The young man stiffened.

Marcus nearly abandoned his plan as a lost cause, but then forced himself to go on. "I am riding out shortly to oversee the planting in the south fields. Perhaps you would care to accompany me."

Lucien's expression betrayed surprise, then wariness. "Y-Y-you are inviting me to join you?"

"Killingworth Manor may someday be yours. You should begin to learn something of its workings if you are to hold it in good stewardship for future generations."

The young man looked as if to refuse, but after a moment he swallowed hard and nodded. "Very well, sir." Then the door swung open and he scrambled out.

The earl slowly followed, hoping that the first seeds or reconciliation were not falling on totally barren ground.

* * *

WAS THAT A ONE OR A SEVEN?

Eliza squinted at the crumpled scrap of paper and tried to decipher the smudged scrawl. Surely seven pinches of willow bark would render the tisane far too potent.

But perhaps not.

With a resigned shrug, she decided to lay it aside until her sister returned from the herb garden. Meredith would know the right amount, for despite her youth, she already possessed a knowledge of the healing arts that left even the elderly village midwife shaking her head in admiration. *Fever, coughs, chilblains, sprains*—whatever the ailment, the locals had learned to come around to the Kirtland cottage for advice.

Even as a child, Meredith had shown a remarkable aptitude for helping those in need. She had often accompanied their father on his rounds through the countryside, learning how to deal with all manner of illness or injury. Over the years, she had also compiled a vast collection of home remedies. As Eliza surveyed the growing stack of neatly transcribed recipes with some satisfaction, she reflected on what a wealth of information lay before her. Surely some publisher in London would recognize its value and consider putting its pages into print.

She tucked the pen behind her ear and took a moment to polish her spectacles. Even if the finished manuscript were rejected out of hand, the challenge of putting together the compendium of healing recipes was well worth the effort. A sense of purpose had kept Meredith from dwelling too deeply in despair. Oh, there were still intermittent cries in the night, and several times she had spied a tear in her sister's eye when the younger girl had thought no one was looking. But barely a week had passed since the attack and Meredith had already begun to venture outside again, if only within the confines of their own walled gardens.

So although her sister had yet to regain her usual sunny laugh or resume her daily foraging for wild plants, there was reason for feeling sanguine. Her passion, like that of any artist, seemed to have given her a certain inner strength with which to brave through adversity.

The thought brought a ghost of a smile to Eliza's lips. Meredith was, indeed, as much an artist with her healing herbs as

Wordsworth was with his lilting words or Gainsborough with his deft brush.

While she, on the other hand, was merely the practical one, the useful one.

Useful. Hardly an adjective that inspired admiration.

A knock at the front door recalled her from such musings. Straightening her apron, she wondered who could be calling. Between planting and shearing, there was nary a neighbor who was not occupied with some task until supper. Nor were they so far in arrears at the butcher that Mr. Withers would send his boy around with a request for payment.

Edith, their aged housekeeper, ventured to poke her head into the parlor. "Begging your pardon, Miss Kirtland, but there is a gentleman who wants to see Miss Merry." From the purse of her lips, it was clear that she was undecided on what to make of the visitor. "I thought it best to bring him here to see you instead."

Eliza nodded, growing even more mystified. There was more than one farm lad who would stop by on his way home from the fields to visit with her sister—usually on the pretext of procuring some remedy for a family member. But never at this hour. And with their homespun clothes and callused hands, none of them could ever be mistaken for a gentleman...

The latch clicked.

Dropping her spectacles, she yanked open the desk drawer and grabbed for the hidden pistol.

The door had closed behind him so the young man had nowhere to retreat. He regarded the barrel pointing dead at his chest and swallowed hard.

"I—"

"You thought you might find her alone again?" The hammer drew back with a loud click. "There may only be females in this house, but rest assured, we are not as defenseless as you apparently think. As I told your uncle, I am accorded to be a good shot. And I would like nothing better than to put a bullet in your heart."

Eliza paused, her eyes dropping a touch. "Or perhaps in some other part of your anatomy. Then we won't have to worry about you accosting innocent young girls ever again."

Lucien hesitated, but after drawing a ragged breath, he ventured a step forward. "I—I brought these for your sister." He held out a bouquet of delicate wildflowers entwined with fronds of curling fiddlehead ferns.

Eliza could only stare in disbelief.

Awkward and embarrassed, he let it fall back to his side. "What I meant to say was, I wish to inquire how she is feeling..."

"How is she feeling?" Eliza finally found her voice. "You assault her, and then think to offer her a posy?" The smooth steel was cool and inviting against her fingers.

One squeeze.

Tempting though the thought was, she kept a grip on her anger. "Your devilish uncle must have introduced you to opium as well as brandy during your carousings in London. Only that would explain the madness that has seized hold of your brain."

Lucien recoiled as if struck. "I am truly sorry for what happened. I don't understand how I could have turned violent!" A bit of greenery slipped from his fingers. "I shall never allow myself to become foxed again," he added softly. "Never!"

"That is hardly of any solace to my sister," replied Eliza, but something in his voice stopped her from further sarcasm. The barrel of the pistol slowly angled away from his chest. "You are not welcome here, sir. Do you really think that any amount of money or silly fripperies can buy you forgiveness for your crime?"

His eyes pressed closed. "No. Not forgiveness, but perhaps..."

A sudden breeze stirred the forgotten flowers as the door to the garden came open. Meredith, her arms filled with a basket of cuttings, stopped on the threshold and drew in a breath. The bruising around her eye had faded considerably, but it still stood out against the ivory pallor of her skin. Like a dark cloud lingering at the horizon of a luminous sky.

Lucien cleared his throat, but his voice came out as barely more than a whisper. "These are for you, Miss Meredith." He glanced down at the fragile blooms, then suddenly let them fall to the floor. "Good Lord, what a complete looby I must appear! Forgive me."

He stepped back, fumbling for the door latch. "Forgive me." With that, he hurried from the room.

Meredith continued to stare, first at the gaping door, then at the tangle of flowers. Slowly she set aside her basket to gather them up. "I should put these in water," she murmured, handling them with great care. "Else they will wither and die."

"Let them," growled Eliza as she moved to return her weapon to the drawer.

"No, I shall not punish them for a crime they did not commit." She put them carefully atop her cut herbs. "I think...perhaps Mr. Harkness truly regrets what he did."

Eliza scowled. "You are much too kind and forgiving, Merry."

A faint twinkle came to her sister's eye. "I'm sure Papa would have told us that is the proper Christian sentiment, would he not?"

"Then I am a heathen," she muttered. "Or at least it is the Old Testament that is more to my taste. I confess, I was sorely tempted to pull the trigger while my weapon was aimed at his nether region. An eye for an eye—or in this case, some other part of the gentleman's anatomy."

Meredith colored slightly, but couldn't repress a smile. "You *do* have a bit of the avenging prophet in you. Though in truth, it is more a classical Deity—like Diana the Huntress—that you remind me of." She sighed. "Poor Mr. Harkness did have the look of a creature being cornered by some relentless pursuer.

"*Beast* is a more apt moniker."

Her sister fingered a bud of larkspur. "Is it?" she asked in a soft voice. "On the few occasions that we chanced to meet during the past few weeks, he was always very courteous and, well, rather sweetly shy. It is hard to believe he is entirely evil. I mean, he does seem to be genuinely remorseful."

"Because you yourself are so good, you find it hard to believe that anyone else is capable of deliberate cruelty. But you must take my word for it, there *are* such people. And many are pampered young gentlemen who are used to getting whatever they what."

The drawer closed with a bang. "The world they live in is entirely different from ours. So it is best to stay as far away as possible from the likes of Lord Killingworth and his nephew."

It was a warning meant as much for herself as for Meredith.

Five

The earl put down his pen and rubbed at his bleary eyes. Lud, the figures were making his head ache far worse than any keg of spirits ever had. Try as he might, he found it impossible to make sense of the endless columns of estate expenditures, or to decide whether they were all necessary.

Bloody hell. Somehow he would have to figure out which ones might be put off. Even though his proficiency in mathematics was rudimentary at best, it took only a simple schoolboy's skill to see the costs were far exceeding the income.

His lips pursed. Was this endeavor to restore Killingworth Park to its former glory just as corkbrained as some of his past stunts? At least some of those other whims, like racing his yacht to the Orkney Islands, or wooing away the Duke of Derwitt's buxom mistress, had had some element of excitement to balance the danger. This current undertaking, however, offered nothing but a dull, unrelenting sense of being slowly sucked under by the morass of responsibilities.

He supposed it should not have come as any great surprise that the estate was in such a sorry state. Successive generations of Killingworth earls—himself included—had contributed to its demise by frittering away its wealth rather than ploughing it back into the land. It was his grandfather who had first abandoned the rolling fields and rugged cliffs for the pleasures of Town. His father had also preferred the life of a boisterous bon vivant to that of a bucolic farmer. Marcus doubted the man had ever set foot in the once-elegant manor halls. Rather, he was content to spend its ever-dwindling profits at the faro tables without risking a thought as to how the estate was being managed. The rich farmland had slowly grown over with thistle and thorns. Only a few scattered sheep now grazed the hills—hills once alive with flocks of fat, black-faced merino ewes and rams that yielded some of the most prized wool in England.

Marcus looked down once again at the sea of fiery red upon the page, each individual number seemingly a taunting rebuke to his casual neglect. He had shown no more care for the ancestral seat than his forebearers. The truth had hit home six months ago, during a meeting with his man of affairs in London. The fellow had informed him that the prudent plan of action was to put the vast estate up for sale since the Greeley coffers, while not exactly empty, were no longer in any shape to bear the burden of its losses.

The news had forced him to take yet another sobering look at his life. In doing so, he realized that he didn't wish to be the one to let the land—a heritage that had been in his family's possession since the time of William the Conqueror—slip through his fingers.

It had been humbling to face the fact that he had accomplished precious little to be proud of over the course of thirty years. His spirits, already blue-deviled for some time, had teetered on the brink of black despair until it suddenly seemed that he might make amends for a lifetime of wasted chances by taking on the challenge of Killingworth Park. He had already given up his heavy drinking and carousing, so there was little reason not to abandon London as well.

The decision made, he had closed up his townhouse in a matter of days and set off for the country, determined that this time his efforts would result in something more meaningful than a scribbled line in a betting book or a furtive coupling in a garden.

Now, however, the earl couldn't help but wonder if his best efforts would be anywhere good enough.

How in the devil had he been such a naive fool as to imagine he might have the knowledge or the experience to run a vast estate?

Marcus glumly thumbed open yet another ledger. The sort of talents that had earned him such a high regard in London were of no matter here. Who cared whether his cravat was tied in a perfect Waterfall or whether his box step was a picture of precise elegance? That he was a bruising rider and skilled with his fives might earn him marginally more respect, but on the whole, he felt utterly useless.

Why, he didn't even know enough to judge whether his steward was halfway competent or whether the fellow was stealing him blind.

A harried grimace twisted his mouth, and after a cursory examination of yet another page of incomprehensible numbers, Marcus snapped the book shut. Setting it back atop the stack still waiting for his perusal, he pushed away from his desk and decided to quit the task for a while, before his mood became too black. After all, he reminded himself with a humorless smile, there would be plenty of time to continue later on, for it was not as if there was much other entertainment to choose from.

Restless, Marcus prowled through the empty corridors, passing by a number of rooms that were still gloomy with dust and Holland covers. On the stone terrace off the music room, he stopped to light up a cheroot and watch the sun set. But rather than take any real pleasure in the subtle play of pinks and mauves against the deepening blue of the evening sky, he found himself making a mental note to ask the housekeeper the cost of hiring another maid. And whether such an addition would have any noticeable effect on the daunting amount of cleaning yet to be done.

Tossing the half-finished cheroot aside, he moved on to the library, thinking perhaps a glass of brandy and a book of poetry might help to keep the feeling of overwhelming bleakness at bay. A fire had been lit and the soft flicker of the flames made the leather spines and gold-leaf titles glow with a mellow warmth. His spirits brightened a bit as he approached the carved oak shelves. Tracing a hand along several rows of books, he took his time in choosing a slim volume wedged between two tomes on the natural history of the Americas.

It was not until he crossed to the sideboard that the earl realized he was not alone.

"Sorry, sir." The high back armchair scraped over the carpet as Lucien shifted uncomfortably and lay down his own book. "I had thought you were busy in your study. I'll go upstairs—"

Marcus motioned for his nephew to stay where he was, suddenly finding that the prospect of dialogue with aught but the demons in his own head was not entirely unwelcome. "No need for that." He poured himself a splash of brandy. "Care to join me?"

The young man blanched and shook his head.

The earl set aside the decanter and took some time to settle himself in the facing chair before speaking again. "Do you mean to give it up? I must warn you, many men find such a resolve impossible, no matter how hard they try."

"In truth, I rarely care to imbibe more than a glass," answered Lucien softly. "I have little taste for it, sir." A ragged sigh followed. "And my senses even less tolerance, it would seem."

The earl's brows rose in surprise. "Yet you rode out each night to get jug bitten with your friends?"

Lucien bit at his lip. "I—I thought perhaps you might like me better if I was more like you."

Bloody hell. Marcus closed his eyes for a moment. Yet another careless sin for which he bore blame. It had never occurred to him that the young man might consider him a hero of sorts and try to emulate his less than exemplary behavior.

"Is that why you chose to join the Wolf's Head Club?" A small and exclusive society of gentlemen, its members included some of the wildest blades of the *ton*. Marcus did not consider himself easy to shock, yet even he found some of their activities went beyond the pale.

"I was invited because of my connection to you, sir, and I hoped to prove I was not a man-milliner," admitted Lucien. After a small swallow, he went on in a tone of near awe. "Your exploits are near legendary. And though I could never hope to match your prowess in—"

"Hell's teeth, don't remind me of all the idiotic things I have done," exclaimed the earl, more roughly than he intended.

His nephew flinched.

"I am not angry with you, Lucien," he added quietly. "It is my own self with whom I am sorely disappointed."

"But..." The young man looked thoroughly perplexed. "I don't understand."

Marcus raised his glass to dancing flames of the fire and slowly swirled the amber spirits. The light refracted off the cut crystal and churning brandy, sending a kaleidoscope of patterns across the dark paneling.

"No, I don't imagine you do," he murmured.

"It is hard to fathom what you might find lacking in yourself, sir. While I..." Lucien let out a harsh laugh. "I have no need to plumb any great depths to find my own faults."

"We all make mistakes—"

"None so grievous as mine," cried his nephew with some bitterness.

"Yours was serious, but as long as you truly regret the transgression and do your best to make amends, that is all you can ask of yourself."

"I do regret it!" The young man leaned forward to bury his

head in his hands. "I still have trouble believing I could act in such a violent way, no matter how foxed I was."

The earl pursed his lips. "I have seen spirits spark even the most mild of men into a flaming temper. Do you know exactly what it was that set you off?"

"No! That's the devil of it. I can't remember a thing." Lucien looked up, his face taut with self-loathing. "You would think I should recall *something* of ravishing a young lady."

"Unfortunately there are times when the amount of drink renders you completely insensible to what you are doing. I was lucky enough to escape such lapses of judgment without paying any more of a penalty than a bilious stomach and an aching head."

"Yes, I have heard much of The Black Cat's luck," murmured Lucien, with his first hint of a smile.

Marcus gave a wry grimace. "Much exaggerated, as indeed are most of the stories."

"Nonetheless, I should like to hear some of them," said his nephew shyly. "That is, if you wouldn't find it too much of a bore to spend time with me."

"I suppose there are one or two that would bear repeating sometime." He rose to put another log on the fire, surprised to find he had no urge to return to the solitude of his study. As he stirred the coals to flame, Lucien stood up abruptly and began to pace before the hearth.

"This afternoon I rode over to see...*her*."

"Did you?" Finishing the task, Marcus leaned back against the mantel and regarded the shadowed planes of the young man's profile. "Hmmm. You have more courage than most, to risk facing the elder sister. I'm amazed you returned unscathed."

Lucien pulled a face. "Well, she did pull a pistol—"

A bark of laughter cut off his words. "She seems rather fond of that damn thing. And you managed to avoid a bullet in the breast?"

"Actually, the threat was aimed a bit lower on my person."

The earl had to stifle another deep chuckle. "Sorry," he said, his lips still twitching with amusement. "Having served as her target myself, I know it is not quite so humorous to be facing those molten green eyes."

"Green, sir? It is you who showed courage, sir, if you were able to remark on the color of Miss Kirtland's eyes. I'm afraid my attention was wholly occupied with the steel-gray orb of the weapon."

Marcus grinned in answer, then his expression became serious. "It is rather our adversary who exhibited a steady nerve. And trigger finger. For that, I suppose, we should be grateful, else neither of us would be in any condition to make light of the experience." He paused to watch the log suddenly catch fire. "A singular female, indeed. Though not one I wish to encounter again any time soon."

That was not entirely true, Marcus was forced to admit as he watched the sinuous sway of the flames. Although it ran counter to all reason, there was something about the heated intensity of the lady's gaze that intrigued him. And not simply because she had taken it into her head to undress him on their first meeting. He felt a slight tightening of his body on recalling the scene—well, maybe that *had* added a certain spark to things. As did the memory of her willowy curves pressed up against his bare chest. Despite the unladylike language and actions there had been no doubt that the figure beneath the thick wool cloak was very much a female.

Grimacing, the earl sought his chair and pushed it back from the heat of the hearth. No doubt he was entertaining such absurd fantasies because it had been so long since he had enjoyed any intimacy with a woman. He would soon have to consider a visit to Town, for he had no intention of giving the local tabbies—and the tigress—any reason to embellish the rumors of his amatory exploits.

"Aye, sir, Miss Kirtland has a real fire about her," mused Lucien, as if he had been reading the earl's thoughts. "Yet one can hardly blame her for reacting in such a way. I, for one, can't help but admire such spirit, even though she would just as soon see me boiled in oil. She obviously...cares very much for her family and would do anything to protect them from harm."

Perhaps it was his imagination, but Marcus thought he detected a note of wistfulness in his nephew's voice. "Loyalty is indeed a noble sentiment," he murmured.

His nephew sighed. "Well, after this afternoon, she not only thinks me a veritable monster but a complete idiot as well."

The earl arched his brows in question.

"I...I brought flowers to Miss Meredith." The young man colored slightly. "That was terribly stupid of me, wasn't it?"

"Is that a rhetorical question, or do you really wish my opinion?"

"Oh, I should like very much to know what you think, sir," answered Lucien.

The look that lit his nephew's face caused Marcus to feel as if a fist had been planted in his gut.

Hell's Teeth, it was just another painful reminder of how blind he had been. No, he corrected himself. Blind implied that he was not able to see. What he had been was self-centered, not blind. And damnably selfish to boot.

He took a long sip of his brandy to hide his unsettled feelings. Suddenly, he felt woefully unqualified to offer advice of any sort, but at the same time he realized that silence would only be worse.

"Sometimes a simple gesture is more eloquent than any carefully planned speech," he answered.

Lucien appeared to be considering the words from all angles as his head tilted slowly from side to side. "I hadn't thought of it like that," he finally said. "But what you say makes a great deal of sense." He added a shy smile. "Thank you, sir."

The young man's grateful expression did much to assuage the dull ache in the pit of his stomach.

"With your reputation of nerve and daring," he went on haltingly, "I don't imagine you ever made a cake of yourself."

Marcus thought about the stack of ledgers on his desk and decided they could wait. What was happening here was worth infinitely more than any of the pounds and pence contained within their covers.

He settled down more comfortably into soft leather of the armchair and stretched his legs out toward the fire. "Oh, as to that..."

* * *

THE VISITOR CAREFULLY SCRAPED THE MUD AND CHAFF from his boots before stepping into the freshly swept entrance hall. "Is Mrs. Kirtland feeling any better today, Miss Eliza?" he inquired, remembering at the last minute to remove his wool cap.

"Yes, she appears a good deal stronger, though my sister is still a bit concerned about the inflammation in her lungs." Eliza brushed a limp curl from her cheek. "It is kind of you to stop and ask, Ned."

"Well, I doubt that there is a fancy medical man in all of London who would be better able to care for her than Miss Meredith," replied her neighbor. By the momentary flicker of his gaze, Eliza saw that her pinched features and subdued tone did not escape his notice. However, when he cleared his throat, it was only to offer her a small burlap sack. "I brought you an extra dozen eggs and a pint of fresh milk in case you might like Mrs. Derwood to fix a custard for your mother's supper."

"How thoughtful." Eliza took the package without further comment, hoping to discourage him from lingering at their door. She had no wish for company, especially his. Despite his roughcut appearance, her neighbor had proven himself to be a sharp, observant man.

At the moment, however, he appeared oblivious to her hint. Instead of taking his leave, he merely shuffled his weight from foot to foot. Short of being suspiciously rude, she had little choice but to answer his hospitality. With an inward sigh, she gestured toward the little parlor. "Would you care to come in for a cup of tea?"

"Aye, that would be right nice."

"Why don't you have a seat? I shall just be a minute in taking these back to the kitchen."

When she returned, her neighbor was perched precariously on one of the ladderback chairs, which looked in danger of collapsing from the weight of his solid bulk. A wisp of a smile crossed her lips. "I think that you might be a touch more comfortable on the sofa, Ned."

The farmer gave a baleful glance at his wrinkled trousers and worn jacket, the evidence of a day spent plowing the fields still clinging to the homespun cloth. "Oh, but Miss Eliza, I wouldn't want to go sitting on your proper furniture in such a state."

Her smile became more pronounced as she surveyed the faded chintz and lopsided frame. "I think it has survived far worse than any assault by your person. Do move, else I shan't have a moment's peace wondering whether I shall have to summon Meredith to treat a broken leg. And I mean yours, not the chair's."

He got up reluctantly and settled himself on the edge of the sofa cushions while she took a seat in the facing chair. His massive hands, which looked more like those of a pugilist than a farmer, twisted at his cap as he fixed her with a probing gaze.

"If you don't mind me saying so, you are looking quite peaked, Miss Eliza, which isn't at all like you."

Eliza *did* mind. But instead of making any retort, she dropped her eyes to her apron and began to smooth at the creases. "My mother's illness has naturally been of great concern to me of late."

"Naturally." There was an awkward pause as he shifted his position. "I have missed seeing Miss Meredith out on her usual walks to collect plants. I hope she isn't feeling poorly as well?"

There was a veiled urgency to his question that caused her own hands to fist in her lap. "You know Merry is never ill," she replied lightly, trying to appear unconcerned.

The arrival of the housekeeper with the tea tray gave her an excuse for saying no more than that. Trying hard to disguise her sense of relief, she thanked the woman and began to busy herself with pouring the brew and cutting a generous wedge of the warm apple cake.

Ned Laskin, however, refused to be put off. "Aye, it's true she never seems to suffer from any fever or cough, but 'tis a nasty bruise she is sporting on her face."

Eliza's hand gave a jerk, nearly spilling the cup she was passing to him.

"Happens I caught sight of her out back as I came in from the fields," he went on in a low voice. "Is anything amiss here, Miss Eliza? I would hope you would consider me a close enough friend to confide any...trouble."

"Merry slipped and took a bad fall on the rocks down by the abandoned mill," she said quickly, hoping to put an end to such questions.

The waggle of his bushy brows conveyed quite clearly what he thought of her explanation. His reply, however, was a bit more oblique. "Hmmph. Never known Miss Meredith to be clumsy, either."

"Accidents do happen, Ned, no matter how careful one is." Her voice was rather more shrill than she intended, and she sought to temper the tone with a forced smile. "Living on a farm, you know that as well as anyone."

"Aye." He took a moment to add several spoonfuls of sugar and a slosh of cream to his tea. "It's odd, that's all, that the vicinity of Chertwell is proving more than a mite dangerous to pretty young females of late," he murmured.

Eliza felt the blood drain from her face. "Whatever do you mean?"

Ned's cup hovered in front of his lips. "Will Yount's daughter was attacked last night as she was returning from tending a sick lamb in his upper pasture. Whoever it was roughed her up pretty bad when she tried to resist." His voice became edged with a sharp anger. "And that ain't the worst of it, Miss Eliza, though perhaps I ought not be speaking of such things, you being unmarried and all."

"Nonsense," she responded. "I'm certainly old enough not to be shocked by the ways of the world. Of course you can speak of such realities without fearing I shall fall into a fit of vapors." Her mouth compressed in a tight line. "Poor Mary. Do neither Will nor his neighbors have any idea of who might have done such a horrible thing?"

"No." He took a long swallow of his tea, then fixed her with a searching look. "But you may rest assured that if anyone has any information on who the cowardly dastard is, he'll be dealt with sure enough."

Eliza bit her lip, trying to decide just how to reply. On one hand, she wished to protect her sister. The attack itself had been terrible enough without having Meredith's reputation being bandied about by the local wags. Yet such circumspection warred with the desire to see justice done.

Or was it vengeance? She couldn't help but hear the echo of the earl's words as she pondered her decision. A part of her acknowledged that perhaps justice was best left to the proper authorities. Toying with her spoon, she countered the admission by recalling the bitter truth of Marcus's other words—a title and money had more to do with the magistrate's brand of justice than the right and wrong.

No, this was not about vengeance, she assured herself. It was about stopping a vile monster before he harmed yet another young girl. Good Lord, it appeared he had already struck again, perhaps in part because of her very silence.

To quell any further debate with her conscience, she also reminded herself that Ned Laskin was a man of solid character, and well-respected within the village. Surely there was no harm in letting drop certain information, so that someone else might help in deciding what ought to be done.

A bit of the cake crumbled in her fingers. Then, mind made up, she finally spoke. "Did anyone note whether the Earl of Killingworth's nephew was seen in the area?"

Ned's eyes narrowed. "You think I should inquire?" he asked slowly.

Eliza chose her words carefully. "I believe there is an old saying in one of my father's books that goes something like this—the apple rarely falls far from the tree. Are you familiar with it?"

"Aye. I've heard that one, too." He took his time in finishing off the last of his tea. "Well, I had best be on my way." As his hands carefully folded the cotton napkin into a neat square, Eliza couldn't help but notice that his knuckles were hard and fissured as chunks of granite. "There are things that need attending to."

"Ned—"

"Thank you for the tea, Miss Eliza. And for making the meaning of some of them old riddles more...clear to a simple man like me." He rose and tucked his cap under his arm, not before fixing her with a steady look. "You know, I have always thought you were a female of uncommon good sense."

Six

Meredith lifted her skirts and started to climb over the low stile. The snap of a twig caused her to flinch, but as a grouse broke from a nearby thicket, she forced a rueful smile at her own skittishness and cleared the last step. Just as she had figured, a scattering of mushrooms were poking up within the copse of trees fringing the pasture. Despite the deep shadows playing beneath the overhanging limbs, their speckled caps, still damp from an early afternoon shower, were faintly visible among the thick roots.

The breeze ruffled her hair as she drew in a deep breath. She found herself savoring the cool touch of it on her cheeks and the wafting scent of wet leaves and sunlight, rich with the earthy promise of spring growth. Happy to have made the first steps at recovering her confidence, Meredith moved slowly toward the secluded glade. Heedless of the raindrops still clinging to the bed of moss, she knelt and began to dig out the pale stems.

Another sound, this one considerably louder than the whirring of a bird's wings, suddenly echoed through the woods, followed by a flurry of thrashing steps. Meredith grabbed for her basket, but before she could scramble to her feet, a large shape burst from the tangle of brambles.

"Ohhh!" she cried in some alarm. Then any further words of dismay dissolved into a burble of laughter as the tongue of a shaggy gray hound slobbered a kiss across her nose.

"Down, boy," she murmured, burying her hands deep into the animal's thick ruff to ward off another wet embrace. "I assure you, I have already washed behind my ears this morning."

In answer, the hound wagged its plumed tail and gave a delighted bark.

"Ajax!"

The hairy paws dropped from her chest, not before leaving two muddy prints across the sprigged muslin.

"You needn't be afraid. He's really quite harmless—" Lucien's words caught in his throat on seeing who it was. It took a moment to dislodge the rest of them. "T-that is, he's hardly more than a pup," he stammered. "And, well, he's very friendly."

Meredith was already standing, her fingers still wound in the hound's silky fur. She shrank back behind a small elm as the young man took a step toward her.

He fell back as well, a faint flush stealing to his face. "I-I only meant to stop him from doing any more damage to your gown."

As if on command, the animal wiggled out of her grasp and took the end of her sash in his jaws, giving it a playful tug. Struggling to keep her balance, she couldn't help but smile at the hound's antics.

"It's nothing beyond repair," said Meredith softly, her eyes straying down from her streaked bodice to the bits of moss and leaves clinging to her skirts, then finally to her muddy hem and the waterlogged half boots. "And besides, I'm afraid my appearance was ruined way before the arrival of Ajax."

"Not at all!" Lucien seemed unable to tear his gaze from her tousled gold curls and downcast features. "I mean, nothing about your appearance seems ruined in the least. Y-you look just like one of those ethereal wood sprites one reads about in fairy tales—" His face turned a vivid shade of scarlet as he choked on the rest of his words.

Meredith took pity on his stuttering embarrassment and ventured a step away from tree trunk.

"Don't run away just yet," he cried before she could speak. "Please! I just want to have a word with you, that's all." He shoved his hands into his pockets, as if to confirm he had no intention of laying a finger on her.

She took another step sideways. "I wasn't going to flee. I'm not afraid of you."

"Y-you aren't?"

A ghost of a smile stole to her lips. "I suppose it is on account of the bouquet you chose."

He looked rather confused.

"If you had chosen hothouse roses or some other fancy flowers, it would have been one thing," she explained. "But you brought wildflowers. It seems to me that no man who would go out and gather such a delicate assortment of blooms can be entirely evil."

He stared at his feet, and looked to be debating whether to speak again or to simply slink away with his tail between his legs.

The awkward silence was broken by a playful bark. The hound had taken up a small broken branch and was bounding back and forth between them.

"What a delightful dog. Is he yours?" she asked, taking the stick from his jaws and tossing it to the edge of the field.

"No, he belongs to Uncle Marcus," answered Lucien. Ajax returned at a dead run, this time dropping the stick at his feet. He picked it up and hurled it deep into the tall grass. "But as he lacks the temperament of a proper hunter, he's been banished from the kennels by the gamekeeper. We have taken to spending a good deal of time together." His mouth crooked in a lopsided grimace. "Two strays taking solace in each other, I suppose, since neither of us is considered a credit to our breed."

Surprised by the note of raw hurt in his voice, Meredith stole a peek at his face. There was no trace of the lordly arrogance, only a rather wistful plaintiveness more befitting a lost pup. With a start, she realized she felt no more threatened by his presence than she did by the frolicking hound in the meadow.

"I know you must think me a veritable monster," he said slowly, his voice as pinched as his features. "And no doubt you wish me to the very hottest corner of Hell, but..." He paused in some confusion, his hands raking through his chestnut locks. "Good Lord, to say 'I'm sorry' seems so woefully inadequate. Any words would be, no matter how eloquently I might try to phrase them."

Ignoring the thrust of the hound's muzzle against his thigh, Lucien forced himself to continue. "What my uncle proposed...I want you to know I am more than willing to offer you the protection of my name. Despite what you must think, I am not really a wastrel or a vicious drunkard. I-I can't explain what happened that night, for I don't understand it myself."

He hitched in a deep breath. "But that sort of violence would never happen again, I swear it. I should be a decent sort of husband to you, Miss Meredith. And I should try very hard to make up for the suffering I have caused you."

It took a moment for her to answer. "It is a most generous offer, Mr. Harkness. But you would only be following one mistake with another, I think. After all, we barely have any acquaintance with each other and might soon come to regret such a hasty decision." Her voice dropped to a near whisper. "I, for one, would wish for a better reason than mere fear of scandal to consider marriage. One that includes a mutual regard and affection."

He hung his head.

"But as for your apology, sir—my father was a rector, but not the fire and brimstone sort. He believed in forgiveness. As do I."

"It is you who are the generous one, Miss Meredith." A rueful quirk tugged at the corners of his mouth. "Though somehow I doubt your sister would care to hear you voice such kind sentiments."

Meredith answered with a quick smile of her own. "I'm afraid Eliza feels that she must look after all of us like a protective mother hen, though I am hardly a helpless chick any longer. I'm sorry she flew into the boughs with you."

"I believe it was a furred rather than feathered species that came to Uncle Marcus's mind in regard to your sister—a tigress to be exact." The glimmer of humor disappeared from his face, replaced by a more earnest expression. "But having a loving family is nothing for which to be sorry. Indeed, you are truly fortunate to have someone who cares so deeply for you."

"Have you no siblings, Mr. Harkness?"

He shook his head. Meredith found something in his forlorn expression prompted yet another question from her.

"And your parents?"

Ajax whined and nuzzled his nose against Lucien's hand. The young man squatted down and began to scratch behind the animal's ears, drawing a low *whoof* of contentment for his efforts. "Would that people were so easy to please," he murmured softly. Then, looking up at Meredith, he added, "An outbreak of influenza swept through our estate when I was barely fourteen. I recovered. My parents did not."

"I'm so sorry. That must have been very difficult for you."

He winced. "I did not mean—that is, I am hardly trying to elicit sympathy from you."

Ignoring his halting apology, Meredith continued her gentle probing. "Is the earl your closest family, then?"

"Yes, Uncle Marcus is my guardian. For nine more months, that is."

"Oh dear, that has an ominous ring to it. I gather you and your uncle do not rub together very well. Do you chafe at the fact he holds the reins?"

"Rather it is he who regrets being saddled with the responsibility for a callow youth, and a bookish one at that. At least, I imagine he does. We don't know each other very well, but I can't help thinking I am hardly the sort of dashing fellow he would wish to be his heir. Everyone holds him in the greatest awe, while me— well, you know quite well what should be thought of me."

"Perhaps you are being too hard on yourself. One mistake does not condemn a person for a lifetime."

"You are far more generous than I deserve."

Meredith found herself wanting to bring the smile back to his lips. It was really quite a nice one, she decided, the rugged masculinity of its chiseled contours tempered by a boyish vulnerability that softened any sharpness. Indeed, she had to restrain the urge to reach out and smooth away the look of haunted regret that tugged at its corners.

"If your uncle has any sense at all, he should be quite proud of you," she said in a rush. "It takes a good deal of courage to admit a mistake and be willing to accept the consequences."

His mouth did soften a bit, but before he could manage a suitable reply, she reached down and took up her basket. "It's getting rather late," she observed, her eyes straying to the lengthening shadows around them. "I had best be going home before my sister begins to worry."

The hound, on seeing the basket rise, thought it another game and tried to bury his nose in the mushrooms. She steered him away with a gentle push. "You are a sweet thing, Ajax, but now I must bid you goodbye. And you, too, Mr. Harkness."

Lucien took hold of the animal's collar and watched her hurry away. "I vow, old boy, I shall never let anyone disparage your abilities," he murmured. "You are quite the cleverest dog in all of England."

* * *

"*WHAT?*" EXCLAIMED ELIZA.

Meredith didn't look up from sorting the various plants into neat little piles on the kitchen table. "I imagine that is a rhetorical question, since it seems you heard quite clearly what I just said."

"If I had any idea that scoundrel was lurking in the vicinity," she muttered, "I would have insisted you take the pistol along."

"And a waste of effort it would have been, since I wouldn't have any idea which end to point where, even if I had the desire to pull the trigger. Which I don't. No, I shall leave such extreme measures to you, Liza." She calmly began to separate the mushroom caps from their stems. "Besides, I was not in any danger from Mr. Harkness."

"How can you say that!"

"I can't really explain it," she admitted. "I just...knew."

Eliza rinsed out the last of the teacups. She dried it and put it aside on the washboard before speaking again. "You should also know that Mary Yount was attacked last night," she said quietly.

Her sister turned so pale that Eliza feared she might be in danger of swooning. However, Meredith steadied herself on the edge of the table, and in a moment a bit of color returned to her cheeks. "I do not think that Mr. Harkness is capable of such duplicity. If you had seen him—he was so genuinely remorseful. And nice." The twist of her features showed how desperately she wished to believe her own assertion.

"It seems highly unlikely that there are two such men prowling about Chertwell."

When Meredith made no answer, she went on, though she hated having to strike another blow at her sister's faith in her fellow man. "Merry, things are not always as they seem, no matter how much we might want them to be. Promise me you will stay away from Lord Killingworth's nephew."

There was a noticeable hesitation before the whispered answer. "If it is what you wish, then very well. I shall do as you ask."

It was a less enthusiastic agreement that she might have wished for, but on slanting a glance at her sister's troubled face, Eliza decided it would do for the moment.

* * *

"SIX TIMES TWELVE, MINUS FOUR AND A HALF percent..." Eliza's muttering nearly drowned out the scratching of her pen on the sheet of scrap paper. She paused to add up the figures for a third time before entering them for real in the ledger.

"Hell's bells!" With a guilty grimace, she looked around to see if anyone had overheard her slip of the tongue. Only Caliban, draped in a sinuous curve over the back of the faded sofa, was within earshot and he did nothing more than give a lazy yawn and go back to grooming his whiskers.

Her eyes turned back to the page. After yet another tally she was forced to crumple up the sheet and toss it away. Why her mind refused to function with its usual precision this morning was most puzzling, but rather than risk making a hash of the accounts, she set her quill aside.

A snort of frustration punctuated the slam of her desk drawer. It drew an answering hiss from the other occupant of the parlor. Four paws landed on the open ledger and a twitching tail began to tickle her nose.

"Oh, Cal," she murmured, scratching the cat's chin. "It seems you are the only one of this household about whom I don't have to worry."

The cat blinked in some mysterious feline sign of commiseration and nudged her hand to continue the caresses.

Eliza sighed and kept up her musings as well. "Mama is growing slowly weaker, though her good days disguise the truth. Edith is becoming so frail that she can barely climb the stairs or carry anything heavier than a pillow. And Merry—"

Eliza stopped to chew at her lip. The cat sat back on its haunches and mimicked her action.

"I'm not sure quite what to do about Merry," she admitted.

Caliban answered with a throaty purr.

"Is that so?" Eliza allowed herself a rueful smile as the cat rolled onto his back and began to swat at the ball of discarded paper. "Well, then, I see I should ask your advice more often."

What she dared not say aloud was that her own agitated state of mind was causing nearly as much concern as the worries about her family. "Hell's bells," she repeated, though only in a whisper. And the Devil himself must be ringing the peal.

In this case, the Devil was a tall, raven-haired gentleman with sensuous amber eyes and a lithe, muscular body that would tempt even the most saintly female to contemplate the pleasures of sin.

Well, it was quite clear she was no saint.

Just as there was no denying that her own shameful dreams were dancing to his tune, no matter how hard she tried to banish the image of candlelight flickering across his chest, or of dark curls beckoning her eyes to follow their drift lower and lower...

Why was such a disreputable scoundrel causing her nerves to jangle at the very thought of his touch? Why did the mere recollection of how warm his flesh had felt bring a clanging to her ears and a weakness in her knees?

A faint voice from deep inside ventured to answer. Perhaps because it seemed unlikely she would be pressed up against a man's naked chest any time in the near future.

Or not so near future, she amended, after considering every male of her acquaintance between the ages of eight and eighty.

Rather than taking solace in that thought, the harsh truth of it only served to strike yet another dissonant chord within her.

But where were such maudlin overtones coming from? The thought of spinsterhood had never before bothered her. Indeed, she rather considered the lack of a husband a blessing instead of a curse—one that allowed her the freedom to use her head for something more than merely nodding meek answers in reply to a domineering male. More puzzled than before, Eliza found her gaze wandering to the mullioned window. Outside in the garden, a robin was busy weaving a bit of straw into the foundations of a nest. But somehow the simple harmony of its twittering song sounded dull and flat to her ears.

Dull and flat. An apt description of her present prospects.

She let out a harried sigh as her gaze returned to the ledgers. At least she was useful, she scolded to herself, trying to fill the strange, echoing hollowness in her heart with a flurry of reason. A figure rendered in ink was far more preferable than a figure molded of flesh—no matter how attractive that flesh was. Numbers represented a certain immutable order. Their value was a constant, unaffected by mood or desire. Solid and predictable, they could be counted on to tally up as they should at the end of the day.

And they most certainly didn't knock one's sense all akilter with a sensual smile.

Again her eyes strayed, this time to the crumpled paper between the cat's paws. Just like the plaguey columns crossed out in black, her feelings were refusing to add up as they should this morning. It made no sense that—

Eliza's odd musings were interrupted by a soft knock at the door. "I promised to leave a bottle of my willow bark spirits at the village blacksmith for Mr. Grimsley. Do you wish for me to drop off Mr. Horely's ledger?" asked Meredith. "I shall be passing by his shop."

"No, no." Eliza scrambled to her feet, grateful for an excuse to silence the disquieting ringing in her head. "I could use a bit of fresh air. I'll come with you." She tucked the book of accounts under her arm and went to fetch her bonnet.

As she passed by Meredith, she couldn't help but note that the troubled look of the previous evening still lingered in her sister's eyes, underscored by smudges dark as coal. All thought of her own troubles faded in the face of such obvious distress.

"Oh, Merry," she said, touching her arm. "Have the nightmares returned? Perhaps Buzzing Bess will have something you might take to lessen—"

"No, it's not that," replied Meredith quickly. "I-I am more concerned with Mary than myself. Do you think we might her pay a visit?"

Eliza shook her head. "While she will no doubt welcome your sympathy at some later date, right now I think she and her family would prefer to get through the horror with a modicum of privacy."

Her sister's lower lip quivered just a bit. "I suppose you are right." She made to turn away but Eliza's hand held firm.

"Is that all that is bothering you?"

"I—I am trying to think if there is aught else we need to pick up for Mama. We are running low on clover honey and must not forget to stop by Bess's cottage for another jar. A generous dollop added to hot tea seems the most effective means of easing the cough."

Eliza decided there was little point in challenging the halting explanation, but concern was still etched on her features as she followed the younger girl from the room. It took only a short while to make a quick survey of the pantry and take their leave from the elderly housekeeper, promising to return by teatime.

After a short discussion concerning certain potions and poultices that had yet to be tried for their mother, their conversation seemed to trail off as if by mutual consent. By the time they reached the shortcut skirting a thick copse of trees, the only sounds were the soft scuffling of their steps and the plaintive hoot of an owl from deep within the shadows of the ancient oaks.

Still in a pensive mood from her own mental ramblings, Eliza didn't mind the long lapses of silence. At the moment, however, it was her sister's strange behavior concerning one of the gentlemen from London that occupied her thoughts, rather than her own odd reaction.

How was it that a sensible girl like Merry appeared so reluctant to acknowledge what terrible danger still lurked before her very nose? It was not as if she needed further proof of what such a villain was capable of, and yet she seemed stubbornly set on trusting intuition over incontrovertible evidence. Why, the man had confessed to the crime! How much more proof was necessary to convince her sister that the Black Cat's nephew was not a purring tabby?

A leopard was a more apt description, she decided, all gnashing fangs and tearing claws. Such an animal simply did not change his spots, however soft and cuddly he may appear when not on the prowl.

Eliza thinned her lips to a wry grimace. She was becoming rather proficient at dispensing well-used aphorisms. Perhaps it would be wise to remember her own supposedly sage advice.

A last little sigh signaled her decision to broach the subject with Meredith, no matter that it promised to be a difficult one. But before she could speak, a sharp yelp sounded from among the bushes.

"Why, Ajax!" exclaimed Meredith as a hound bounded up to her side and began nosing in some impatience at her hand.

"I shall be glad to give you a proper greeting, sweeting, if you will stand still for just a moment."

Eliza gave a grudging smile as she watched the animal dance around in a tight circle, then jump up and drag his paws down the front of Meredith's skirts. "The two of you appear to be good friends."

Without looking up, Meredith sought to catch hold of its ruff. "He belongs to Mr. Harkness." The words came out softly enough but there was an undertone of defiance to them that drew another harried sigh from Eliza.

"Oh, Merry, do you really think it wise—" Her words suddenly caught in her throat as she stared more closely at the streak on her sister's gown. Mixed in with the bits of leaves and mud was a swath of rusty red.

"Dear God."

Meredith's eyes flew down to her waist. In some disbelief, she brushed her fingers slowly across the stain and exhaled sharply as they came away covered in blood.

Ajax whined and began to tug at her shawl.

"Show me," whispered Meredith.

The hound made a sound more howl than bark, then broke away and raced into the tangle of brush. Meredith and Eliza were right on its tail, clawing their way through the brambles and vines. They stumbled onto a faint path that led on toward what seemed to be a small clearing among the gnarled trunks. Through the flickering light, Eliza thought she could make out the silhouettes of curling fiddlehead ferns, along with some darker, dimmer shape on the ground behind them.

Ajax gave another agitated bark, causing their steps to accelerate in tandem.

She wasn't sure whether it was Meredith or herself who screamed first.

Seven

The shape was that of a man. A badly beaten man from the look of the goodly amount of blood soaking the disheveled curls and ripped coat. Half hidden by the undergrowth, he lay face down, one arm twisted under his chest. There was no sign of movement, not even when the hound gave a doleful whine and nudged his nose against the crooked knee.

"Dear God," repeated Eliza, feeling as if she, too, had been struck a violent blow. Though the face was not yet visible, she had a queasy feeling that the features were going to prove all too recognizable, despite the awful battering.

A low cry was the only sound from Meredith. Taking the last few steps at a dead run, she sank down beside the man's prostrate form and took gentle hold of his shoulders.

Eliza tried to peel her sister's hands away. "Let me see to him," she demanded, hoping to spare Meredith what promised to be a horrible sight.

"No!" Even as she spoke, Meredith was already working to turn the body face up with as much care as she could. "I don't need to be protected, not from this."

Sensing that no amount of arguing would do any good, Eliza

fell silent and concentrated her efforts on helping raise the body out of the mud.

It was worse than she had feared. Beneath the matted locks, the man's eyes were so pummeled as to be swollen completely shut, and his cheeks were puffed to nearly twice their normal size with deep, purpling bruises. The nose, smashed at an odd angle, was still oozing a trickle of blood that tinged the split lips a viscous red.

Meredith managed to choke down a retch, but her teeth could not keep from chattering as she unwound the torn cravat and sought for a sign of life.

Eliza forced a calmness that belied the churning of her own insides. To her vague surprise, her vocal chords cooperated and her words came out with an eerie flatness. "Is he dead?"

It was a moment before her sister was able to answer. "There is a slight pulse, but it's very weak." She raised her eyes. "I know what you think of him, but we cannot just walk away and leave him to die, Liza. We must get help!"

"I never meant—" She caught herself, realizing this was hardly the time to debate the finer points of her feelings. "Of course we must get help. And have word sent to Lord Killingworth." Her gaze jerked back to the pitiful face staring up at them with bruise-battered eyes. "I don't suppose there is any doubt that this is his nephew?"

"It is Mr. Harkness—I recognize the signet ring on his finger. And the c-color of his hair." Again, Meredith nearly broke down in a sob after slanting a look at the blood-soaked curls, but quickly regained control. "You must run to the village while I stay with—"

"No, I will stay here and you will go," countered Eliza.

"I hardly think Mr. Harkness poses any threat at the moment!"

"It is not Mr. Harkness I am thinking about, but whoever has done this to him!" She indicated the reticule by her side. "Unlike you, I do not consider it wasted effort to lug around a hunk of iron. Nor will I hesitate to use it. I'll not let any more harm come to him, so cease brangling with me and go!"

To her relief, any further argument seemed to die upon Meredith's lips. After no more than a moment of hesitation, she scrambled to her feet and set off toward the lane as quickly as the way would allow.

Ajax seemed torn between whether to follow her or stay behind. He trailed along for some yards, then returned to his adopted master. With a plaintive *whoof*, he stretched out at the fallen man's feet, so close that his muzzle was touching the outstretched boot.

"We'll not let any more harm come to him, I promise," murmured Eliza in response to the look of mute appeal in the hound's mournful eyes. A sigh of her own joined the soft growls. "For all the good it will do him now."

Forcing her gaze back to the bruised face, she busied herself with wiping the worst of the mud and blood from the wounds. There was little else she could do, save bandage several deep lacerations on his hands with strips torn from her petticoat and cover him with her shawl.

And to offer up a silent prayer. To her surprise, Eliza found she was doing just that.

It seemed like an age before the sound of voices and a wagon approaching on the rutted lane announced that help had finally arrived.

"Here!" she cried in answer to a muffled shout.

Meredith appeared in a matter of minutes, followed by three men. "Is he still…"

"Yes, he's still alive," replied Eliza. She stood up, glad to relinquish her place by the young man's side to the local physician. Ajax looked up sharply, but made no protest as Mr. Dawkins began a quick assessment of the injuries.

The words he muttered were inaudible but his grim expression made his feeling clear enough as he examined the extent of the damage. "As nasty a piece of work as I've ever witnessed," he announced, looking up from Lucien's bruised body. "I'll do what I can, but..." The rest was left unsaid. After a moment he added, "Any idea of who would do this to the earl's nephew? And why?"

The other two local men averted their eyes and made no answer.

Eliza also remained silent, praying that her sister would not make any hasty revelations. A spasm crossed Meredith's face, but she merely bit her lip.

"Hmmph." The doctor gave them all another searching look, then wasted no more time on reflection. "Bob and Josiah, go fetch the boards from the back of my gig. We must move him carefully if we are to avoid further damage. Miss Meredith, if you will go with them and bring back my medical bag, while Miss Kirtland helps me lift..."

His gruff commands set everyone into action, and in short order Lucien had been carried out to the lane. As the three men lifted the makeshift stretcher onto the pile of straw, a rider thundered into view from around the bend, his mount spurred to a furious gallop. Before the lathered stallion came to a full halt, Marcus was out of the saddle and running to his nephew's side.

One look at the battered face caused the blood to drain from his own visage. Drawing in a sharp breath, he turned to engage in a terse conversation with the doctor. What he heard caused his expression to harden and Eliza heard him curse as he stepped forward to help the two men in strapping down the board.

When the task was done, the doctor scrambled up beside his patient and motioned for the other men to take charge of the reins.

The earl watched the gig until it disappeared around the bend, then turned to the two sisters. His mouth was compressed in a tight line, lips near white with the force of his shock and outrage.

His gaze locked on Eliza, his amber eyes afire with a molten swirl of emotion. "Well, Miss Kirtland..." In contrast to his look, his voice was very cool and its note of weary bitterness caused a lump of ice to form in the pit of her belly. "Are you now satisfied that justice has been done?"

* * *

"Is there any news?" asked Meredith softly.

Eliza put down her reticule and removed her bonnet before making an answer. "Mr. Giles says Dr. Yount was still at the manor when his boy delivered the requested medicines, but...Mr. Harkness had not regained consciousness." She unpacked the items she had brought back from the village and laid them out with great care upon the kitchen table, hoping to forestall any further questioning. "I trust I have not forgotten any of the things you asked for."

"No, it appears everything is here." Meredith continued a methodical grinding until the piece of willow bark in her pestle had been reduced to a fine powder. She then laid the mortar aside and wiped her fingers on a dish towel. "There is something else, isn't there? Something you wish to keep from me."

There was, but Eliza knew it was pointless to deny it. Her sister would hear of it soon enough. "Apparently Dr. Yount has tried to hire someone skilled in nursing to tend to the young man, but no one in the area will take a position at Killingworth Court, not even Sadie Fathing, who is desperately in need of money."

Ignoring Meredith's gasp of surprise, she added," Indeed, two of the housemaids have already quit, due to the...rumors."

"But—but if Mr. Harkness does not have the proper medical care, he may die!"

Eliza felt her mouth thin to a grim line. "Quite likely. And townsfolk are saying it would be good riddance. They hope such a dire event might also drive the cursed Black Cat away from these parts."

"And you, Eliza? Is that what you say, too?"

Eliza was rendered momentarily speechless by the look in her sister's eyes. It was as if a sudden squall had darkened the normally placid blue into a sea of stormy slate.

"Do all of you really believe you have the right to decide who should live and who should die?" continued Meredith in an agitated voice that was equally at odds with her usual sunny calm. "I cannot imagine, even for an instant, presuming to possess such wisdom."

The words forced Eliza to confront the image of twisted limbs and face beaten to a pulp. All at once she felt the bile rise in her throat, and for a precarious moment she feared she might be physically sick. Her sister's question—as well as the earl's thinly veiled accusation—implied she was playing God. Had she in some way usurped the role of the Almighty in pointing a finger at the one she had decided was guilty?

"Neither can I," she whispered, taking her head between her hands. "Believe me, I know I am all too human to sit in judgment of others. What happened was wrong, no matter what crimes the young man has committed."

Without a word, Meredith untied her apron and went to the still room. When she returned several minutes later, a basket filled with an assortment of jars and crocks was in her arms.

Although Eliza feared she knew the answer, she could not help but ask, "What do you mean to do?"

Glass clinked against glass as another bottle was taken down from a shelf and added to the load.

"Meredith, your intentions are noble, but you cannot go to Killingworth Manor."

"I cannot, in good conscience, stay away when I know I have the skill to help. The earl is in desperate need of someone to move in and tend to Mr. Harkness until he is recovered."

"Move in—are you mad? It can't be done! Not without causing utter ruin to your reputation."

Meredith's chin rose in a defiant tilt. "Is a reputation worth more than a human life?"

"Do you wish to live the rest of your life as a reviled outcast?" countered Eliza.

After a moment of strained silence, Eliza added, "Both questions are much too complex to answer with a simple yes or no." She pushed back a lock of hair from her forehead. "Oh, Meredith, you are guided by lofty principle while I am the practical one, who considers the harsh realities of the world."

"If you were to come with me—"

Eliza shook her head. "I would hardly be considered a proper chaperone, since I am also unmarried and not quite of an age to be thought above temptation. I'm sorry, but as we are not related to the earl, the idea of spending any time under His Lordship's roof is simply out of the question. "

There was a heavy silence, save for the scrape of an earthenware jug against a pine shelf. "But if it were known that I was...engaged to Mr. Harkness, that would quiet any gossip, wouldn't it?" said Meredith slowly, her words quite firm despite the fact that they had been uttered in barely more than a whisper. "Especially if you came along. And...and Mama, too, for naturally she could not be left alone here."

"Good Lord." Eliza drew in a deep breath. "You are serious, aren't you?"

"We could say that we were waiting for Mama to recover her health before making the announcement public, but that given the seriousness of his injuries, our family felt beholden to show its support." She added a bundle of dried herbs to all the other things she had assembled. "Even the worst of the tabbies would be hard pressed to find fault with that."

"And when the young man recovers—if he recovers?"

Her sister gave a tiny shrug. "Mr. Harkness would return to London, and after a suitable length of time, I could simply announce that I have decided we would...not suit.

"I suppose it might work," admitted Eliza, noting the look of grim determination etched on her sister's pale features. "But I cannot imagine the earl will like such a mad idea any more than I do."

* * *

"YOU ARE PROPOSING *WHAT*?" ASKED MARCUS.

Eliza pulled her shawl a bit tighter around her shoulders. "Come along, Meredith. I told you His Lordship would not agree to any such arrangement."

Her sister, however, refused to be pulled away from the massive oak door quite yet, despite the fact that several oaths had preceded the question. "I realize it is not the most ideal solution, Lord Killingworth, but to be blunt, there are precious few other choices. Dr. Yount did not exaggerate—you will find no one willing to come tend to your nephew. And by the time you can arrange for any help to be sent down from London, it may be too late."

The earl folded his arms across his chest, finding his initial anger turning into a grudging respect as the delicate slip of a girl did not wilt under his sharp scrutiny.

As if sensing a softening of his initial opposition, Meredith pressed on. "Not to speak of the fact that the sort of women sent out as nurses by an employment agency are usually more likely to steal a tipple from your supply of brandy than to offer competent care for your nephew. While I, on the other hand, am accorded to have some skill in the healing arts."

"So I have been told." His lips pursed as he considered the highly unorthodox proposal. "You are truly willing to do this?"

Meredith nodded.

His eyes swept to Eliza. "And you are truly prepared to go along with it?"

Her chin rose a fraction. "As my sister said, it is the right thing to do, sir."

He muttered something under his breath, then let out an exasperated sigh. "Then I should be fool—or worse—to decline your offer of aid. Yount has already informed me that he must leave here within the hour, for there are other patients in dire need of his attentions."

"I came prepared to stay, sir," said Meredith quickly. "If you will have someone take me to your nephew's chamber, I will go over with Dr. Yount what he wishes done."

"And I will go on to the village and begin spreading the felicitous news," muttered Eliza, with a good deal less enthusiasm. "Perhaps, if I am lucky, I can keep the flames of wild speculation from burning us all to a crisp."

Stung by the sarcasm in her tone, Marcus found it impossible not to reply with equal sharpness. "You needn't make it so clear that you think you are descending into the bowels of Hell," he growled. "Believe me, I am no more happy than you are about the devilish turn of events, Miss Kirtland. It is, after all, my nephew who lies at death's door, and no matter that the entire shire seems to think he deserves to roast in eternal damnation, none of you had the right to act the avenging angel."

He noted with some measure of satisfaction that his words had brought a tinge of color to her cheeks. "If I were not in agreement with you on that, I would not be here, sir," Eliza replied stiffly. "But you are right—since it seems we are going to be forced into close proximity for a while, we should strive to be civil with one another."

Noting the fire that was still smoldering in her eyes, he could well imagine how difficult a task that was going to prove for the young lady. As well as for himself. They seemed to rub together like flint and steel, setting off sparks at the slightest contact.

"If you would be so kind as to send your carriage around in several hours, sir, I will have a trunk packed and my mother ready to be brought here," she added with scathing politeness.

He gave an exaggerated bow.

"I should really make haste to join Dr. Yount," murmured Meredith in a gentle reminder as she, too, watched her sister stalk off in a swish of skirts.

"Yes. Of course." Forcing his gaze away from Eliza, the earl stepped aside and gestured for her to enter the Manor. "I will have my housekeeper—assuming I still have one—show you up to the sickroom."

The hawk-faced woman in charge of the staff was none too pleased at having to make preparations for three female house-guests, especially with the shortage of help. By the time Marcus had managed to sooth the ruffled feathers and retreat to the sanc-tuary of his library, it was he, and not some slatternly nurse, who was ready to steal into the supply of brandy.

But despite the temptation to drown his growing frustration in a bottle of spirits, the earl reminded himself with a baleful grimace that he had better keep a clear head. He couldn't begin to guess at what other crisis might arise before the day was over—though how it could get any worse was difficult for him to imagine.

Taking up a poker, he jabbed at the banked fire, fighting back a feeling of raw helplessness. He could strike back against an enemy that had a name and a face, but against a swirl of rumor and innuendo...

A low oath mingled with the crackling coals. It appeared that the Black Cat's legendary luck had finally come to the end of its nine lives. His decision to remove to the quiet of the countryside had only resulted in one disaster after another. Perhaps the locals were right in seeing him as an omen of misfortune, he thought glumly as he ran his hand through his locks. Perhaps he brought nothing but grief to anyone whose path he crossed.

Supper that night did very little to dispel his dark mood. Miss Kirtland's notion of civility seemed to be based on keeping her mouth firmly shut, save for a peckish nibble or two at her food. And as Meredith partook of only the first course before rushing back to the sickroom, the rest of the meal was passed in a gloomy silence, save for the scrape of silver on the heirloom china. He couldn't have been more relieved when the plates were finally taken away by the lone footman and the young lady had excused herself to tend to her ailing mother.

Marcus sought refuge in his study, but after pouring a glass of brandy he suddenly felt the need to escape from the house and drink in a breath of fresh air. The night was damp with the lingering chill of a passing shower, yet it was not nearly as oppressive as his own clouded thoughts.

Bloody hell—what a muddle.

Lighting a cheroot, he leaned up against the terrace railing and blew out a ring of smoke. It caught in a puff of wind and drifted out toward the gardens, only to melt into the mist in the blink of an eye.

Life was just as ephemeral, he mused, thinking of Lucien hovering between this world and the next. As were hopes that went with it.

And dreams.

Had he ever had dreams? His jaw tightened. Or merely whims and desires?

A light mizzle started again, but the earl ignored the moisture beading along the arch of his brows and pooling in the hollows of his cheeks. Would that it would drown out such disquieting questions. Had his own life really been as meaningless as he feared? All things considered, he could not in truth say that anything he had done so far was of any more substance than a fleeting breath of tobacco-warmed air.

With a slight shudder he ground out the sodden stub beneath his boot and went back inside.

* * *

"How is he?" asked Eliza.

"His pulse is still very weak, but as of yet, no fever has set in." Meredith looked up from folding a length of clean linen. In the flickering candlelight, the smudges of fatigue beneath her eyes looked much the same as the bruises that mottled her patient's face. "I managed to get several swallows of laudanum down his throat, so right now there is little more I can do but wait."

"Get some rest. I'll sit with him for a time." Eliza removed the fabric from her sister's fumbling fingers and helped her rise. "You will be of no use to anyone if you are muzzy with fatigue."

"But you have been tending to Mother all evening," protested Meredith.

"As she has been sleeping soundly, I was able to lie down for a bit. The move does not appear to have upset her unduly. Indeed, the news of your...betrothal has, if anything, brought a pinch of color back to her cheeks."

Eliza's words caused a dull flush to rise to her sister's face. "I hope she will not be too...disappointed when it is broken off," came the soft response.

"Let us not worry about the future. There are quite enough problems in the present to keep us occupied."

A tiny smile played briefly on Meredith's lips. "As you say, always the practical one. You are right, of course." She stood up and rubbed absently at the back of her neck. "Promise you will rouse me the moment there is any change. And—" A light kiss brushed Eliza's cheek. "—thank you. I know how much you disapprove of this, but I am grateful for your sacrifice."

Sacrifice, repeated Eliza silently as her sister left the sickroom. She wished she might claim her presence was due to any such noble sentiment. But it wasn't. It was due to guilt—pure, simple, and selfish. She was not here merely to help nurse the young man's grievous injuries but to salve her own conscience.

Lucien stirred, a faint groan interrupting his ragged breathing. The blanket had fallen away and his profile lay in shadowed contrast to the white pillow. She stared for a moment. With his thick lashes fluttering against his pale cheek, he looked very young and very innocent. Hardly the face of a vicious criminal.

But appearances could be deceiving, she reminded herself with a reluctant sigh. Especially as she had every reason as of late to question her own judgment.

Guilt. Innocence. Would any of them involved in this sordid affair atone for their sins?

She was not sorry to be distracted from such musings by the opening of the door. "Surely you cannot mean to return—"

But it was the earl, not Meredith, who stepped into the room.

"You need not worry," she added wryly, seeing his gaze move sharply from the glass in her hand to his nephew's lips. "It is not hemlock, but a soothing potion that my sister brewed. We must try to keep any fever from developing."

His only answer was reach out and lay his hand lightly on Lucien's brow. Eliza noted with some surprise how lithe and strong his fingers appeared, and yet how gently they brushed at the young man's hair. "His forehead feels deucedly hot."

"Yes." She dipped a piece of felt in the basin of cool water and wrung it out. "All we can do is bathe his face and try to get him to swallow the medicine. After that, I'm afraid nature will have to run its course."

Marcus looked as if to say something, then remained silent as his touch trailed down to the bandaged cheek.

"Rest assured that my sister and I will see to it that he is not left untended."

"You think I will rest while he lies here in suffering?" he snapped. "Go to your own bed, Miss Kirtland. I will take my turn by the sickbed, if you will but show me what I must do."

"But—"

"But what?" His dark brows drew together in a formidable scowl, and as he leaned forward, Eliza was suddenly aware of the heat emanating from him as well. It was enough to bring two hot spots of color to her cheeks, though she wasn't quite sure why.

"You think me devoid of all sensibility? Incapable of caring what happens to my nephew?"

"N—not exactly," she stammered, taken aback by the raw edge

in his voice. In truth, she *had* thought him coldly arrogant and unfeeling in his treatment of everyone, including Mr. Harkness. Now, however, she could see how wrong she was to imagine there was naught but ice water in his veins. His gaze held a simmering intensity that caused her breath to catch in her throat.

"It's just that from what I observed, there did not seem to be much love lost between you and your nephew," she added.

"Perhaps things are not always as they seem, Miss Kirtland."

As the same thought had recently crossed her own mind, she made no retort. But still, at that moment she was sure there was no mistaking was she saw—among the emotions swirling in the depths of his hooded eyes was one that she recognized all too well.

How strange.

For what reason was the Earl of Killingworth feeling guilty?

Too tired and confused to make any sense of it all, Eliza wrung out the strip of flannel. "Perhaps," she answered aloud.

Without further comment, she showed the earl what to do, then rose and took up her candle. "You have only to ring the bell if you need assistance. My sister will relieve you in an hour or two."

He waved her off, and Eliza stumbled toward her room, wishing that when she awoke in the morning, this would all turn out to be a bad dream.

Eight

The magistrate shuffled his feet. "And no clues have been found around the area as to who might be responsible, not even a clear boot print," he continued. "Mayhap when Mr. Harkness regains consciousness, he will be able to tell us something of his attackers." His tone, however, did not indicate that he put a good deal of faith in such hopes.

Marcus allowed his mouth to dip into a sardonic curl. "And of course no one saw anything out of the ordinary."

"It is a deserted stretch of lane," replied the man defensively. "And a time of day when most people are at work in their fields. I will continue to make inquiries."

"Please do," answered the earl with chilling politeness before letting the door fall shut with an audible thud. It was, perhaps, a childish thing to do, seeing as it came within a hair's breadth of knocking the fellow flat on his arse. But no doubt planting the insincere little toad a facer—which he had been sorely tempted to do—would have been worse.

Not that it mattered a whit whether he begged or ranted or threatened. The man might make a show of going through the motions of a real investigation, but it was a sham. Everyone, himself included, knew that no culprit was going to be charged in the beating.

Still, he would have liked to wipe the smug surety from the fellow's expression, if only for an instant.

He turned to stalk off toward his study, so caught up in muttering imprecations against the local authorities that he nearly collided with Meredith as she came down the stairs.

"Has Lucien taken a turn for the worse?" he demanded sharply, noting the tautness around her mouth and the shadows under her eyes.

"Oh, no, sir." She shrank back from him, her gaze dropping down to the basket of herbs in her hands. "He is much the same, though I am concerned about how restless his movements have become. I am going to the kitchen to make up another type of draught, in hopes that it may effect some relief." After a moment of hesitation, she continued past him, her cautious movements reminding him of the way a mouse would sneak past a lurking tabby.

Marcus turned and fell in step beside her. "Forgive me for snapping—my manners have been sadly lacking as of late."

His lips pursed on realizing just how surly his moods must appear to her. No wonder she seemed to think him an ogre.

Or worse.

He cleared his throat and added, "Why, I have not yet even expressed the proper gratitude for your extraordinary kindness, especially given the circumstances..."

"Please don't apologize, milord. You have every right to be upset over what has happened to Mr. Harkness. I am only doing what any responsible person should—"

"Hmmph." The earl interrupted with a low snort. "Not one in a thousand people would exhibit your compassion. Or courage. You are a remarkable young woman, Miss Meredith."

A crimson flush colored her face.

Seeing that he had embarrassed her, he swore under his breath.

Meredith backed away until her shoulders brushed up against the wainscoting. "I—I am really quite ordinary," she stammered. "And unlike Eliza, I am not at all brave."

Realizing that his curses and scowl were only making him appear more intimidating, the earl gave a harried sigh. "Yes, I have no doubt that your redoubtable sister would charge through the gates of Hell if she felt it necessary. However, I wish to assure you that despite what you might have heard, I am not the Devil Incarnate." He took a step closer, trying to read her expression. "Come, Miss Meredith, I trust you are far too intelligent to be afraid of me. Contrary to local rumors, I do not breakfast on small children or ravage innocent girls—"

His words cut off in a strangled choke. How in the name of Lucifer had he blurted out such a tactless remark? "Good Lord, I'm sorry. What a monstrous thing to say…"

Her face finally tilted up towards him and the earl was amazed to see a wry smile flit across her features. "Lord Killingworth, contrary to what my sister—and you—seem to expect, I am not so fragile as to shatter into a thousand pieces at the mere mention of my…misfortune. Other people have suffered far worse tragedies. I shall survive."

Her calm words made him feel even more as if he should be consigned to the hottest corner of Hell. If this mere slip of a country girl could face adversity with such fortitude, what right had he to whine about his own trifling difficulties?

"You put me to blush, Miss Meredith," he said quietly. "In light of your remarkable pluck and spirit, the rest of us appear too blinded by our own weaknesses to see the world so clearly." He clasped his hands behind his back. "A pity in every respect that my nephew did not make…wiser choices. He would be a very fortunate young man if this sham announcement had any truth to it."

Meredith's eyes widened slightly. "B-but Mr. Harkness can look to make a match in the highest circles of Society."

"Having spent many years among such circles, I assure you

that a title and fortune is often quite worthless in itself." The earl caught himself, hoping that the note of bitter regret in his voice did not cause the girl any more confusion than she must already be feeling. "Forgive my odd mood—no doubt I am frightening you." He stepped back. "I should not detain you any longer."

She made no move to slip away. "I am not frightened by you, sir. Despite the rumors about your past, and the fact that you can appear quite a...formidable presence, I believe you to be a very kind and honorable gentleman at heart."

He blinked in surprise.

"Although," she added softly. "It would seem you don't wish for that to be known."

Before he could think of any response, she had slipped past him and turned the corner of the kitchen hallway.

* * *

Eliza paused by the stairs and tucked a lock of hair behind her ear. Her mother looked to be resting comfortably, now that Meredith's medicine had eased the hacking cough. Mr. Harkness, too, appeared to have taken a slight turn for the better. As both patients were likely to sleep through the night, there looked to be no reason why she should not seek her own bed.

Yet despite the lateness of the hour, she did not feel quite ready to retire. Despite the rigors of the sickroom, she found herself missing the challenges of her own daily routine—her books, her papers, her projects. On the morrow, she would have to see about having some of them brought over from the cottage. In the meantime, however, perhaps there was something of interest in the earl's library to serve as a bit of bedtime reading.

Her lips pursed in a wry scrunch. After all, she knew from her previous nocturnal foray that the place did contain a large collection of books. Surely the earl would not begrudge her the loan of a volume or two.

She hesitated, wondering whether to venture another visit to the Black Cat's private lair. The first one had been, in every respect, a rather embarrassing experience. But as a glance below showed nothing but darkness, she decided there was little likelihood of another midnight encounter.

Especially if she were quick about it.

The library door was already slightly ajar. Anxious to be done with the errand, Eliza shouldered it open, taking no notice of the faint glow of candlelight dappling the threshold.

"Bloody Hell and damnation."

The oath was hardly more than a whisper, but it stopped her dead in her tracks. "Oh!" she exclaimed in some dismay. "Forgive my intrusion. I had no idea—"

Marcus looked up, a harried expression on his lean features. The gold-rimmed spectacles perched on his nose blurred the sharpness of his gaze, making him look far less forbidding than usual.

"My words were not directed at you Miss Kirtland," he muttered. "Is something amiss?"

"No, no. I was not yet sleepy, so I, er, I thought I might borrow a book. To read." To her annoyance, Eliza found herself stuttering like a schoolgirl. "That is," she added stiffly, "If you have no objection."

He gave a curt wave at the shelves. "Take whatever you please." Without so much as another glance in her direction, his eyes dropped back to his blotter.

Much as she wished to slink away, she didn't wish to give him the satisfaction of thinking her intimidated by his presence. Drawing in a deep breath, she marched on, but on passing his desk, she couldn't help but glance at what was causing his brows to furrow in such an odd manner.

"You are doing sums?" she murmured on seeing the open ledger. "I wouldn't have thought such a task would have a gentleman like you burning the candles until dawn."

"Actually," snapped the earl, his voice edged with sarcasm. "I am writing a manual on the seduction and deflowering of innocent maidens."

She felt an uncomfortable heat spread over her cheeks. "So much for the notion of civility between us. I'll leave—"

"No, wait." He rubbed at his forehead. "Forgive me. I did not mean to be rude." His mouth crooked in a rueful grimace. "It's just that these columns of numbers are proving to be a more formidable opponent than Napoleon's Imperial Guards."

Did the man actually have a sense of humor?

Her interest piqued, Eliza leaned in to have a closer look. "You have made a mistake," she murmured after a moment.

His brows shot up. "Where?"

"Here." She pointed it out. "Oh—and here." After studying the page a bit longer, she made a face. "Good Lord, you've really made a mull of it. Here, let me have a closer look." Without thinking, she reached for the ledger.

Marcus leaned back without protest and allowed her to take it.

Rather surprised at his willingness to relinquish the accounts to a female, she carried the heavy volume to a nearby chair and began thumbing through the most recent entries. It was quite some time before she finally looked up and called him over.

A series of rapid-fire questions followed, none of which the earl could answer with any certainty.

"Hmmph." Eliza frowned she snapped the covers shut. "It doesn't make any sense. Your estate should be highly profitable. Have you considered switching to wheat in the south fields?"

"Ahhh..."

"And the price you are getting for wool," she went on. "Either your steward is a hopeless incompetent or..." The sentence trailed off, but there was no doubt as to where it was leading.

Marcus's lips thinned. "I was beginning to wonder as much, despite my total lack of knowledge in these matters."

Once again Eliza found herself amazed at his reaction. Most males of her acquaintance would rather swallow nails than admit to any weakness, especially in the face of a female. She cleared her throat. "Unlike you, sir, I have a good deal of experience with the business of farming. If you like, I could have a look at all the past records and see what other irregularities may turn up. I am accorded to have a very good knack with figures."

The earl hesitated, and her faint smile hardened to a brittle scowl. No doubt his next words would be a snide comment concerning females and figures.

"I would be quite grateful," he began, but on taking in her change of expression, words cut off in a harsh laugh. "Ah. It appears you didn't expect me to take you up on the offer. No doubt with all the other duties you have been forced to assume these past few days—"

"It's not that. I—I was simply surprised that you don't mind asking for help from a female."

"I'll take any help I can get. It is clear that males have no innate skill at this." The lopsided smile that tugged at his lips caused Eliza's fingers to go rather slack on the leather binding. "At least not this male."

Hell's bells! Did he practice that boyish expression of vulnerability in front of the looking glass each morning, knowing what a devastating effect it would have on any female close by?

Even an aging country spinster.

Ignore the dratted man, she warned herself, forcing her gaze away from the sensuous curves of his mouth and the twinkle of humor that softened the glitter of his eyes. He may be unskilled in practical subjects like mathematics, but the Earl of Killingworth obviously knew how to slather on the charm.

Finally mastering her momentary confusion, Eliza muttered a tart reply. "Well, I suppose I shall have to credit you with some shred of natural intelligence. Precious few gentlemen are smart enough to realize they are not infallible, much less admit it aloud."

This time, his low laugh held real amusement. "I am well aware of my faults, Miss Kirtland. And if I had, perchance, forgotten even a one, your cataloguing of them over the past few days would certainly have jogged my memory."

Eliza flushed on recollecting all the accusations she had hurled in his face. She ducked her head, pretending to take one last look at the ruled pages. "If you leave these accounts out in the morning room, I shall give them a careful study after breakfast."

With what she hoped was an expression of cool composure, she rose slowly and turned for the door, determined to make a dignified exit.

"Did you forget something?"

Her toe caught on the carpet, ruining the effect. With a silent oath, she looked around in consternation.

"A book—I believe you wished to borrow a book." Marcus gestured at the expanse of shelves. "There are, as you can see, a great many to choose from."

Was the earl really engaging in a bit of banter?

Angry with herself for allowing his rich baritone drawl to send a flutter through her insides, she snapped a waspish retort. "Any suggestions? Or are you as unfamiliar with them as you are with your ledgers?"

Ignoring the obvious sarcasm, Marcus steepled his fingers and appeared to be giving the barb serious consideration. "That would, of course, depend on your tastes, Miss Kirtland. If you favor the classics, there is a wide selection of Homer and the ancient philosophers in both Greek and English—though I'd not recommend the translation of *The Iliad*. It's rather dry in comparison with the original."

There was a fraction of a pause. "Or perhaps the Bard is more to your liking. There is a lovely set of the complete tragedies and comedies." His mouth betrayed a twitch of amusement. "Including *The Taming of the Shrew*."

"Hmmph." She turned on her heel, hoping her cheeks were not quite as burning as they felt. "On second thought, I find I have had enough entertainment for the evening. Good night, sir."

"Good night, Miss Kirtland."

As she drew the door closed, Eliza could have sworn she heard a very unlordly chuckle.

* * *

MEREDITH'S BROW FURROWED AS SHE SPONGED HER patient's face. The fever had returned, bringing a sheen of sweat to Lucien's sunken cheeks and causing his sleep to become more and more fitful. Laying aside the damp flannel, she coaxed a swallow of willow bark tea down his throat, then sought to reorder the tangled bedding. Turning back the sheets, she smoothed out the rumples, but as she began to plump the pillows she noted that his thrashings had brought him perilously close to the edge of the bed.

She hesitated, wondering whether she should summon someone to help lift the young man to a more comfortable position. To manage it herself, she would have to wrap her arms around him in a rather awkward—and intimate—embrace...

A faint groan made her feel ashamed of such qualms.

She slid her hands under Lucien's arms. Despite his slender build, he was a heavier burden than she imagined and it took a good deal of maneuvering to get his limbs straightened and his body shifted to a more settled position. In the process, however, his nightshirt was pulled off his shoulder, baring a good deal of chest.

Meredith quickly reached out to tug it back in place. Well aware of the impropriety of the situation, she kept her eyes averted as much as possible. Still, she could not help but catch a glimpse of the tattoo emblazoned on his breast.

A gasp caught in her throat. For an instant she could only stare in stunned silence at the distinctive design. Then, recovering from her initial shock, she quickly pulled the fabric up to cover his flesh.

"Dear Lord." The words came out as a ragged whisper. Bowing her head, she pressed her palms to her brow.

"Merry!" Eliza's voice was shrill with alarm as she hurried through the door. "What is it? What is wrong?"

She turned, her face leached of all color.

"Good Heavens! You look as if you have seen a ghost."

"No, nothing like that—though the sight of it may haunt me for some time to come." she said rather shakily. "What I have seen is...the truth."

Eliza quickly placed a hand upon sister's brow.

"You needn't fear that I have turned feverish or am suffering from hallucinations. What I meant was, I've just discovered why Mr. Harkness does not remember anything about the night I was assaulted..."

* * *

Marcus listened in grim silence while Meredith repeated her explanation.

"Are you absolutely positive about this?" he demanded. Asking her to relive the incident yet again was not something he wished to do, but one mistake, however honest, had already led to grievous consequences. If at all possible, he wanted to avoid making another, with all of its own unforeseen ramifications.

"Given the circumstances," he added, "it would be quite understandable if some of the details had become confused in your mind."

Meredith did not flinch under his piercing scrutiny. "I am not confused, sir. Not about this. My attacker had a tattoo on his *left* breast, not his right. So Mr. Harkness could not have been that man. He is innocent."

The earl's fingers stilled their drumming. "A pity this conclusion was not reached a trifle earlier," he muttered, unable to keep the edge off his words. On seeing her face twist in remorse, he immediately regretted his sharpness. The rebuke was meant more for her older sister—and, if truth be told, for himself. If both of them had acted with reason rather than anger, then perhaps...

Eliza had so far refrained from comment, but on hearing the implied reproach, she was quick to speak up in her sister's defense. "It is hardly fair to blame Meredith for what has happened. If you recall, sir, it was you who presented your nephew to us as the culprit."

As if he needed to be reminded,

"Although you seem to have difficulty in adding two and two," added Eliza. "I would have thought you could tell left from right."

Damnation. Did the emerald-eyed tigress never sheath her claws? Despite the provocation, he reacted with only a touch of sarcasm. "Had I realized your sister's description was meant to be taken literally, Miss Kirtland, I would have subjected Lucien to a more thorough physical examination. I was aware that he bore a tattoo that matched the one she described, and the chances of two men in this vicinity having the same one seemed awfully low."

Taking up a pen, he said, "You see, I may not be able to add two and two, but I do have a great deal of experience in figuring out the odds. I would have been willing to bet my entire fortune that such a thing was impossible." His tone became even more mocking. "Apparently I would have lost my shirt. That is, assuming the cards were not fuzzed."

The earl was gratified to see the pugnacious expression on Eliza's face turn to one of consternation.

"Figuratively speaking, of course," he went on. "As what we are discussing is hardly a game."

"Just what are you implying, sir?" she demanded

"You claim to have a great skill in mathematics. If you take a moment to calculate the probability of two men in this shire having identical tattoos—which is, by the by, the mark of a very exclusive gentlemen's club in London—I imagine you will figure it out."

"Are you saying that someone deliberately set out to frame Mr. Harkness?" exclaimed Meredith. "How...how very monstrous."

"Indeed." Marcus leaned back in his chair and steepled his fingers. "But then, we already know we are dealing with a monster."

"Someone must have a great deal of enmity for your nephew to go to such extremes to see him discredited," said Eliza.

"Oh, come, Miss Kirtland. While you may think me a witless worm, I give you credit for a possessing a more than average intelligence. Lucien is hardly more than a boy, and one who has led a rather quiet life up until now. I think we both know it is not he who is the real target of these scurrilous rumors and innuendo."

She didn't answer right away, but the earl noted that the color of her eyes had darkened to a near emerald hue. *Emeralds. Tigers.* What was there about the damn woman that kept bringing to mind thoughts of the exotic?

"W—what do you mean, sir?" stammered Meredith.

Marcus turned and gave her a chilly smile. "It would seem that your sister is not the only one dead set against the idea of me taking up residence in Sussex."

Try as she might, Eliza was finding it hard to focus on the scrawled columns. It seemed that the ink had taken on a mind of its own, refusing to stand at attention in an orderly row of numerals. Instead, the squiggles of black kept curling into the outline of an aquiline nose, a set of chiseled lips, a fringe of long sable lashes that no gentleman had a right to possess...

With an exasperated oath, she snapped the ledger shut. Were her eyes equally at fault when it came to looking at other things?

She gave a slight shake of her head. Surely not. The Earl of Killingworth's transgressions were as well documented as the numbers on the lined pages.

And yet...

Eliza slowly thumbed back to the beginning of the section on wool production and spent the next half hour going over each entry with a fine tooth comb. Then once again the covers fell closed in her lap. If her eyes—and her judgment—were so sharp, why was it that nothing was adding up right?

Lips pursed in thought, she reached for a sheet of paper and a pen.

A low cough interrupted her work. "Miss Kirtland, you needn't feel obliged to spend the whole day trying to make sense of those blasted accounts."

She looked up. "That's the trouble, sir. It *doesn't* make sense. Look here—" The tip of her pen pointed to the top of her notes. "To begin with, the price your steward is claiming to have received for sheared wool is but half of the going rate. Now, look down this column."

Marcus peered over her shoulder. After a moment or two, he muttered an oath. "So the sheep are not the only dim-witted creatures who are being fleeced."

"Correct. And I'm afraid that's not all."

He pulled over a chair and sat down. "It gets worse?"

"Much." Eliza turned to the section on rye and oats. "The cheating becomes even more blatant here. And I've yet to analyze the expenses recorded for upkeep of the tenant cottages." She made a face. "*That* should prove an interesting list."

Marcus rubbed at his jaw. "It would seem your low opinion of me is entirely justified."

She was not so sure...

"The devil take it. Such egregious neglect of my responsibilities is criminal."

"You should be taken to task for ignoring such a prime estate as Killingworth Manor," agreed Eliza. "But it is your steward who is guilty of the true crime. I would guess from these numbers that he has been altering the accounts for some time."

The earl grimaced and swore under his breath. "I shall file charges with the magistrate this afternoon—" Catching her frown, he paused in mid-sentence. "You do not advise such a course?"

"It would be a long and drawn-out proceeding," replied Eliza. "And though the numbers do not lie, they can be made to tell more than one story if one is clever enough. I fear that your man is enough of a snake to be able to wiggle out of the accusations. No doubt he has a plausible explanation for each transaction."

She forbore to add that a trial might prove to be highly embarrassing as well as inconclusive, but the earl seemed to read her mind.

"Making me look even more the fool." A lock of dark hair had fallen across his forehead, softening the angular planes of his countenance. For an instant, all Eliza could think of was that he looked far from foolish.

"Well then," he continued, jarring her from such musings. "What would you suggest?"

"Turn your present steward out this instant," she replied without hesitation. "And replace him with an experienced overseer. Someone who is both highly skilled and highly trustworthy."

"The first part is easy enough, but as to the second..." His mouth thinned. "I would think such men would be scarce as hen's teeth.

"Even scarcer."

"That's awfully encouraging," he groused. A harried sigh echoed the rustle of the pages. "So, any idea where I might look?"

"As a matter of fact, I do." Eliza folded her hands atop the ledger. "The candidate I have in mind is scrupulously honest and highly knowledgeable in all the latest advances in agriculture. Furthermore, when given free rein to run things, this person has quickly turned a profit from even the most incompetently managed estate—and usually lowered expenditures in the process." She paused, not looking up. "You will, of course, wish additional references. I can provide you with a list of the local gentry who will corroborate my words."

"If what you say is half true, these services will no doubt cost me a pretty penny," murmured the earl.

She shook her head. "No more than the going rate."

"Ah. A fellow who is noble in both spirit and deed." His dark brows arched in faint amusement. "And just who is this paragon of perfection?

Eliza allowed a tiny smile. "Me."

* * *

"You?" It took a moment for Marcus to realize that his jaw was nearly buried in the folds of his cravat.

"Yes. Me," repeated Eliza calmly.

"The devil take it," he exclaimed. "I would look worse than a fool if I hired a female to run Killingworth Manor—I would look like a Bedlamite!"

"And why is that?"

"Because...because...bloody hell, I think you know quite well why."

"Yes, of course I have heard the reasons. *Ad nauseum*, I might add," she answered, making no attempt to disguise the bitterness in her voice. "All the specious, self-serving arguments that men have used since the time of Adam!" The ledger dropped onto the side table with a pronounced thump. "It is I who belong in Bedlam for thinking that you might be open to reason."

So much for strategy. Somehow, she had him on the defensive again.

"Now, that is not quite fair, Miss Kirtland—"

A snort of derision cut him off. "What isn't fair, sir, is that I am not given a chance to prove my ability, no matter that you are in dire need of help and I have a stack of recommendations attesting to the fact that I am very good at what I do."

"I don't doubt that you are a highly capable young lady—" This time, the abrupt halt in mid-sentence was of his own doing. Ye gods, was he really mouthing such pompous platitudes? No wonder she was looking as if she would like to scratch his eyes out!

Tiger, tiger, burning bright... Contrary to her barb of last night, he was familiar with his books, especially poetry. This was, however, hardly the time to be musing on William Blake, he reminded himself.

Turning his attention back to their skirmishing, Marcus attempted to clear the smoke with a touch of humor. "But be that as it may, I can't imagine why anyone—save for a Bedlamite—would agree to take on the task of dealing with faulty ledgers, fallow fields, sick sheep and moldering grain, no matter what the recompense. I, on the other hand, have little choice but to face up to the muddle."

"It may seem daft to you, nevertheless, it is just the sort of challenge that I would like to try." In the flickering candlelight, he caught a gleam of wetness in her eyes. That they were most likely tears of rage, rather than any show of girlish vapors, caused a twitch of grudging admiration to tug at his lips.

"I may appear odd to you, but I suppose we all have strange notions of what is fun," continued Eliza. "Take, for example, the pursuits you find amusing. I cannot begin to fathom why any sane person would waste his life in such...frivolous pursuits."

He felt the hint of his smile thin to a grim line. "I believe we were discussing your resume, Miss Kirtland, not mine."

"No we weren't," she countered, her gaze once again sparking with indignation. "Discussing it, that is. A discussion implies that the outcome has not already been decided."

Damnation. He tried to scowl, but the sight of her crossed arms and defiant tilt of her chin brought forth a bark of laughter instead. "Very well. Let us abandon hostilities for the moment and assume, for the sake of argument, that I am willing to hear you out, as I would any legitimate applicant for the position. Go ahead and tell me why I should hire you in particular."

She proceeded to do just that. In excruciating detail.

Marcus finally held up his hands in mock surrender. "Enough, Miss Kirtland. I am willing to concede that you are eminently qualified for the job."

"You are?" It was clear his admission had caught her by surprise.

"Yes." Rising from the chair, he moved to the hearth. "But..."

"There is always a 'but,'" she muttered.

A lengthy silence ensued as he took up the poker and carefully rearranged the coals. Out of the corner of his eye, he could see her begin to seethe with impatience at his delay. Still, he made himself reconsider what he was about to say one last time before charging ahead. Perhaps he was insane to entertain the idea. But something about her gritty determination urged him to throw caution to the wind.

After all, what did he have to lose?

"I have a proposition for you—a business proposition," he quickly amended. "It is non-negotiable. You will have to take it or leave it."

Eliza's eyes narrowed. "Go on."

"I will hire you for a position at Killingworth Manor, at whatever salary you deem fair..."

A brilliant smile lit her face.

He cleared his throat, knowing his next words would quickly change the cant of that lovely mouth.

"*But...*"

Sure enough, she was back to looking daggers at him. "But what?"

"But it is not the position you had in mind."

Her brow furrowed.

"You will be responsible for deciding what expenses are necessary, what crops are to be planted, what livestock is to be raised—in short, you will be given full authority to run the estate as you see fit."

"I—I don't understand, sir. That sounds like a steward to me."

"So it does." The earl leaned back against the mantel, taking shameless pleasure in watching the parade of emotions troop across her features. "But I am not hiring you as my steward. I am hiring you as my private advisor, an arrangement that is to remain strictly confidential, else the deal is off." Toying with his signet ring, he added, "I must also warn you that the job will only be a temporary one. Or at least, that is the plan." There was another brief pause as he watched her eyes narrow to slits.

"You see, Miss Kirtland, you are going to teach me how to run Killingworth Manor."

Her response was surprising mild, considering the fireworks he expected.

"If I am to do the job, why can't I take credit for my work and be recognized as your steward?"

"Come now, you are not so naive as that. Given my reputation, how long do you think it would take for all manner of sordid rumors and innuendos to blacken your name once the arrangement became known?"

When she didn't reply right away, he answered for her. "About ten seconds, give or take eight."

"I don't give a fig for what the gossips say."

"Well you damn well should!" he replied, his voice rising. "A reputation should not be handled so carelessly, for once it slips through your fingers, it is gone forever." Aware that she was regarding him with a rather curious stare, he cleared his throat and hurried on. "So use your head and don't be a bloody fool about such things. And don't forget that there is your sister and mother to consider, as well as yourself."

Eliza drew in a sharp breath, but rather than speak right away she rose and began to pace before the windows.

"Let me get this straight, then," she said after several turns. "I will be in charge of devising a plan to make the estate profitable?"

He nodded.

"And you agree to abide by my judgment when it comes to making all the important decisions?"

"You have my word on it. Until such time in the future when we both agree that I am capable of taking charge."

Eliza looked out at the overgrown gardens and distant pasture-lands. "How do I know I can count on you to keep your promise?" she asked warily.

"If we are to work together, I suppose we are both going to have to trust each other." He stared down at his polished Hessians, surprised by how much he hoped that she would. "So, Miss Kirtland, what do you say?"

There was a slight pause. "When do I start?"

"This afternoon. Just as soon as I give Hastings the boot."

* * *

LUCIEN'S EYELIDS FLUTTERED OPEN BUT IT SEEMED TO take a moment or two for him to focus on his surroundings. "Never imagined I would be allowed past the Pearly Gates, but I must be in Heaven as I see an angel..." He sighed as he closed his eyes and shifted on the pillow. "Mmmm. No doubt it is but a dream."

"It is no dream, Mr. Harkness, and you are, thank the Lord, still in the land of the living." Meredith rearranged the coverlet. "I am so glad to see you have finally come awake. We have been very worried about you."

"Miss Meredith! What on earth are you—" Lucien tried to sit up, but fell back with a small groan.

"Oh, don't try to move, sir. You have suffered some very nasty injuries, and although I think the worst has passed, you mustn't tax your strength." She pressed a cup to his lips. "Try to drink a bit of this broth. Then I shall go downstairs and let your uncle know the good news."

"No, please. Don't go just yet," he asked as she made to rise. "I don't understand. How is it that you are here? I mean...." His words trailed off in some confusion.

"You needed care, and I am eminently qualified to give it."

His mouth tugged into a lopsided grimace. "Somehow I doubt it is quite as simple as that. To begin with, what the deuce happened to me? I feel as though a regiment of Boney's cavalry has run roughshod over every particle of flesh and bone."

Meredith regarded him through lowered lashes. "Do you not remember anything about what occurred?"

"No. That is what is so horrible—once again, my memory seems to have failed me. I mean, I do recall walking with Ajax. We were headed toward the village when I heard a voice—a cry, really—coming from the woods. We went to see if someone needed assistance, then..." He shook his head. "Then, everything is a complete blank."

"Just as well," she murmured.

"But what is wrong with me, that I can't recall such things?" His whisper was harsh with self-loathing. "Am I some monster whose mind is addled? Did I attack someone else?"

"Mr. Harkness—"

Ignoring her gentle attempt to interrupt, Lucien became even more agitated. "Good Lord, perhaps Uncle Marcus should have me locked away, before I do any more harm—"

She cut off his recriminations with a touch to his cheek. "Listen to me, Mr. Harkness. You have harmed no one."

He blinked.

"No one," repeated Meredith firmly. "The reason you cannot remember the first incident is because you had no part in it. We have proof of that now. And as for the second one, there is no question that someone attacked you and not the other way around."

She brushed back a lock of hair from his brow. "There is a monster in our midst, but it is *not* you." Her expression turned troubled. "Although the real miscreant is going through a good deal of trouble to make it appear as if it is you."

"That is good news, indeed." A wave of relief washed over his face, yet after a moment, some of the pinch returned to his expression. "But...why me?"

"We have all been wondering that as well. The answer is still a mystery." For the first time, a slight smile came to her lips. "However, Lord Killingworth seemed quite determined to discover who is responsible. And I, for one, would not like to be the guilty party when he does."

"Uncle Marcus?" The young man sounded doubtful. "Can't imagine he would care to expend much effort on my behalf."

"Oh, I think the earl may surprise us all."

*　*　*

"It was on account of the cankers, milord," explained the earl's steward. "Half the herd had to be slaughtered before it was ready for market, to keep the disease from spreading. That's why the profit for mutton is not more for the past season."

"When one spends more on feeding the animals than one gains in selling them, it is not called a profit, Hastings. It is called a loss." Marcus turned to another page of the records. "What about this entry for wheat? I was somewhat surprised at the price per bushel used for the calculations. I was under the impression that the going rate was nearly double what is written down here."

"T—there was a short spell when prices dipped, er, due to a temporary glut in the market. Unfortunately, we had no choice but to sell at the time, else see the grain spoil." The man wet his lips. "A bit of bad luck."

"Bad luck seems to dog your steps, Mr. Hastings. Bad harvests, sick animals, flooded mill ponds, accidental fires, untimely market ventures." Marcus looked up. "Why, another year or two under your hand and my estate may be reduced to naught but barren earth."

"But, sir, the place had been neglected for years. You saw it yourself—the farmlands gone to weeds, the buildings in disrepair, the flocks depleted, the tenants prone to laziness," replied his steward in a wheedling whine. "It takes time to turn things around. If Your Lordship will just have a bit of patience, I have every expectation that the coming season will bring better results."

"So do I," snapped the earl. "For I plan to make a number of changes in the way things are run around here. Beginning with hiring a new steward. One whose efforts will be directed at real improvements rather than in robbing me blind."

The man's mouth went through a number of contortions, reminding the earl of a fish on a hook. "S—slanderous lies, milord! Whoever has been whispering such poisonous words in your ear is naught but a sniveling malcontent. I swear on the Bible—"

"Numbers do not lie. And the only poisonous words are the ones dripping from your forked tongue." Marcus snapped the ledger shut. "You have a half hour to gather your things and slither off my lands, Hastings."

"Y—you are turning me out?" The man gaped in disbelief. "Impossible! I—You can't do that!"

"But I just have. You should be grateful that I haven't called the authorities to haul you off to the jail where you belong. Now get out of my sight, before I change my mind."

The former steward's color went from white to a mottled purple. "You will be sorry," he replied, his voice squeezed to little more than a hiss by a spasm of rage.

Marcus's pen hovered over the blank sheet of paper he had placed on his blotter. "Is that a threat, Hastings?"

The man backed up several steps, then spun around and fled from the room. It wasn't until the door had slammed shut that he dared to turn and spit an answer at the oaken panels.

"Oh, it ain't a threat, Lord Killingworth. It's a bloody promise."

Ten

The earl scratched out the number he had written. "Blast," he muttered. "That can't be right." Adjusting his spectacles, he took a moment to recalculate the column, then penned in a new total beneath the blot of ink.

"Correct." Eliza leaned in over his shoulder. "You see, you are beginning to get the knack of it now."

"I daresay the East India Company will not be vying for my services anytime soon," he replied. "However, as a page of numbers no longer looks like Greek to me, I should be able to tell in the future whether I am being robbed blind."

She turned away from the desk, but not quite enough to hide a half smile. "You read Greek, sir. Fluently."

"And how would you know that, Miss Kirtland?"

Eliza traced a hand over the carved acanthus leaf edging the shelves. She had, he realized, a very graceful hand, long fingered, with a firm yet gentle touch. He watched it come to rest on the top of the book, and couldn't help wondering what her palm would feel like, sliding insides the fastenings of his shirt.

Provocative, he imagined. Just like her intriguing emerald eyes.

Which could be hard as gemstones or soft as the underside of a spring leaf, depending on her mood.

"You make notes in the margins of your books. Rather lengthy ones."

At the moment, her mood seemed quixotic—half serious, half teasing. Was the straightlaced Miss Kirtland actually loosening her hair enough to engage in a bit of banter?

He rather wished she would. The scraped-back curls, wound tight in a prim bun, were particularly unflattering. Not to speak of the slate gray gown, with its choking neckline and long sleeves.

Realizing that his thoughts were in danger of straying into dangerous territory, Marcus made himself return to the subject at hand. "How do you know they're mine, and not those of some long deceased scholar of the family?"

"I recognize your handwriting," replied Eliza. "After all, I've seen quite a bit of it lately, what with having to correct the ledgers and check over the requests you are sending to your bankers."

A low chuckle greeted the answer. "Are you, perchance, thinking of taking up a job as a Bow Street Runner in addition to your other endeavors?"

"I doubt they would pay me nearly as much as you do, sir." Turning in profile, she gazed out the window and the quirk of her lips quickly straightened to an expression that was all business. "Speaking of blunt, I have been going over the costs of repairing the mill, and we may need to ask for additional funds."

Marcus was sorry to see the humor die away from her face. The warmth of a smile, however fleeting, brought a glow to her skin and a sparkle to her eyes that made them appear far richer than cold, hard-edged jewels. A young lady of her years—for she was young, despite her assertions to the contrary—should not always be looking so serious, as if the weight of the world were resting upon her slim shoulders.

A rueful sigh nearly escaped his lips as he realized that he was only adding to her burdens. The job of running Killingworth

Manor was an enormous responsibility to take on, as he was quickly discovering.

Forcing his attention back to the matters of finance, he drawled, "I fear Mr. Countt may suffer a fit of apoplexy when he sees the amount you deem necessary for the job."

"Well, if the coffers are running low, I suppose you could always pay a visit to London and make the rounds of your usual gaming haunts. It is said you have the devil's own luck at the gaming tables, so that should solve the problem."

His jaw tightened. The casual barb sliced through any lingering illusion of camaraderie between them. Surprised at how deeply he felt the cut, he parried with a sharpness of his own.

"I thought you claimed to be far too intelligent to pay any attention to gossip and rumor." After a slight pause, he could not help but add, "And besides, gambling is not quite as simple or predictable as adding or subtracting a column of numbers."

Eliza's gaze remained grimly focused on the distant fields. "I wouldn't know, sir."

"No, I imagine not. You do not strike me as someone who takes any chances in life. Indeed, you are quite as rigid and unbending as one of the neat little numbers you pen on the page, aren't you?"

Marcus removed his spectacles and let his eyes slowly travel from the tips of her half boots to the twist of her tightly coiled bun. "Don't you ever wonder what it might be like to let your hair down, Miss Kirtland, if only for a moment?"

He was childishly gratified to see that his words had brought a flush to her cheeks.

"I will leave my suggestions for the cultivation of the south fields here atop the projection of prices for wheat and rye," she replied flatly. "Do try to study what is there so that you won't be utterly lost when we meet to discuss the project this afternoon."

Slapping the papers down on his desk, Eliza turned for the

door. "In the meantime, I must return to Rose Cottage and fetch a few of my books on agriculture."

"I shall have the carriage brought around."

"Don't bother, sir. I feel in need of a breath of fresh air."

* * *

ODIOUS BEAST. ELIZA KICKED AT A PEBBLE, KNOCKING IT clear across the cart path and into the shallow ditch. How dare the infamous Black Cat assume the right to make such snide assessments of her character! Why, he didn't know the first thing about her. His judgments were based on naught but presumptions...

Hell's Bells.

Another stone skittered through the dust. It was not the same thing, she assured herself, though her toe stubbed on one of the ruts. She knew a great deal about the Earl of Killingworth. Certainly enough to form a valid opinion. He was a jaded rake, who took pleasure in all manner of vice. After all, everything she had heard or read had indicated as much.

Or had it?

She grudgingly recalled the notes written in the margins of *The Iliad.* That he was more learned than she imagined was surprise enough. But his jottings also revealed a sensitive, insightful side to the man she would never have guessed at. And there was no denying that he possessed a lively sense of humor.

With a small snort, Eliza booted yet another projectile through the air, this one ricocheting off the trunk of a gnarled oak. Oh, very well—perhaps she, too, had been a trifle guilty of rushing to judgment.

"Have you taken a dislike to that particular tree? Or is it something else that is troubling you, Eliza?"

Her head snapped up. Framed in one of the stiles was her neighbor, an expression of bemusement mingled with concern shading his features.

"Though I fear I hardly need ask what has brought that dark look to your face, given what you have been forced to endure of late," continued Ned Laskin. Setting aside his pitchfork, he climbed over the rails. "Would that the cursed Black Cat would turn tail and slink back to London, leaving respectable folk like us to live here in peace and quiet."

"He is not quite the devilish creature that you think," she replied tartly, somehow feeling compelled to defend the man.

A furrow came to the farmer's brow. "Don't tell me that you, of all people, have been seduced by his—" The words stuck in his throat as he met her outraged stare. Turning near scarlet, he gave a choked cough. "That is, I did not mean to imply anything...improper. I just meant—"

"I know what you meant, Ned," said Eliza. "And I think you are well enough acquainted with me to know I am not one to be swayed by superficial charm or insincere flattery."

"Aye, you have always shown yourself to possess a great deal of sense." He shoved his hands into his coat pockets and cleared his throat with a cough. "Still, I cannot like the idea of you, or the rest of your family, continuing to stay under that blackguard's roof."

"There is nothing untoward in our visit," she said evenly, though she couldn't quite meet his eye. "Meredith and Mr. Harkness have, as you well know, announced their engagement."

A low oath slipped from his lips. "Forgive me, Eliza, I may be a rough farmer, but I have a grain of sense too. Enough to know a complete bouncer when I hear one."

He fell in step with her. "Why in the name of Heaven are you circulating such a story? I don't understand why you would want to lift a finger to help the earl and his nephew. Especially," he added while slanting her a meaningful look, "in light of recent events."

"I don't need you to remind me of my responsibilities to my family, Ned," she replied tartly. "Nor do I feel obliged to justify my actions. I have my reasons, but that is all I will say at the moment. If you cannot accept that, so be it."

A war of emotions skirmished across his face. Contrition, however, quickly vanquished pique. He came to a halt and took hold of her arm, "Eliza, please. I do not wish to quarrel. If I offended you, it was only out of concern, not malice. I don't mean to question your judgment—"

"Then don't," she said, her voice growing considerably more gentle. Smiling, she reached out and patted his cheek. "I appreciate your concern, but let us say no more on the matter."

"Very well." Reluctance was evident in his tone, but he forced a brisk nod. "Cry friends?"

"Of course. That is, if you will see me home to Rose Cottage." Eliza slipped her arm through his and they continued on along the path. "Tell me, is the change in feed having any effect on how much milk your cows are producing?"

"Aye, your idea proved right..."

The two of them were so engrossed in their discussion of animal husbandry that they didn't notice the approaching rider until he had come abreast of them and reined his mount to a walk.

"Lord Killingworth!" Surprised by his unexpected appearance, Eliza couldn't help but exclaim, "W—what are you doing here?"

The earl gave a curt tip of his beaver hat. "I, too, wished a breath of fresh air, and since I was riding out, I thought I might offer to carry back the books you were fetching from your cottage." His mouth curled into a faint smirk. "However, it appears you have no dearth of knight errants."

Suddenly aware of her arm entwined with Ned's, she stiffened and drew free. "Allow me to introduce my neighbor, Mr. Laskin. We were discussing his...cows." Furious with the earl for making her feel like a foolish schoolgirl, she turned back to her friend and said through gritted teeth, "Ned, allow me to introduce Lord Killingworth."

With the farmer making scant attempt to hide his disapproval, and the earl responding with poisonous politeness, the exchange between the two men was decidedly chill.

"Well, don't let me interrupt your little tete a tete," said Marcus with a mocking smile. "I am stopping in the village on my way back to the manor. Is there anything I might pick up for you, Miss Kirtland?" He cocked a brow. "A fresh supply of hairpins, perhaps?"

She glared at him.

"No? Well then, good day." With the barest of nods in Ned's direction, he spurred his stallion into an easy canter.

"What in Hades did he mean by that?" growled the farmer as he watched the earl ride away.

"Oh, pay it no heed," answered Eliza through gritted teeth. "He has a peculiar sense of humor, that is all."

"Hmmph."

However, a quelling look from her forestalled further comment, and the conversation returned back to milking methods. It continued in that vein until they reached the ivied gate of Rose Cottage.

"You are sure you do not wish for me to wait and escort you back to the Manor," asked Ned, his eyes narrowing as if he has spotted some feral cur prowling among the rhododendrons.

"Don't be silly. I've kept you long enough from your labors, and besides, we are in Chertwell, not the wilds of Egypt or India," she replied, in an attempt to tease the scowl from his face. "So there is really very little danger from lions or tigers."

His expression only darkened. "It's no joking matter, Eliza. Some predator is out there. And I have no doubt he's just biding his time before he pounces again." He tugged at the latch and swung the gate open.

"I am quite sure that neither Lord Killingworth nor his nephew are any threat to this shire," said Eliza softly.

Ned looked at her rather strangely before dropping his gaze to his muddied boots. "I pray you are right." But his face betrayed just how unlikely he thought that was. "You told me a wise old saying from one of your father's books not long ago. Well, I, too, know several proverbs, including this one."

The hinges made a scratchy growl.

"A leopard does not change his spots.

With those parting words, he hunched his shoulders and turned away.

*　*　*

"Shall I stop? You look as though you are growing fatigued."

"No, no, I'm enjoying it immensely." Lucien forced his eyes open. "Really I am. But perhaps you are tired of reading."

Meredith turned a page. "Not at all. What say you we continue on to the end of the chapter? Then I must insist that you get some sleep. Ample rest and nourishment are very important if you are to regain your strength."

Lucien's grin looked almost normal, she noted with satisfaction. The herbal compresses she had applied had brought down the swelling of his lips considerably, and the bruises had faded to dull smudges. "Good Lord, if Cook keeps stuffing me with egg custards and cream porridges, what I shall gain is so much weight that my legs will likely snap from the strain. Do you think I might be allowed a simple slice of beefsteak or a mutton chop?"

"Perhaps a bit of boiled fowl." She smiled at the look of distaste that puckered his features. "Then, in a day or two, if your condition keeps improving at such a rapid pace, we will see whether you are able to rise for a short spell. I am a firm believer in the idea that getting the limbs up and moving helps speed a patient's recovery. Once you can manage that, you may have whatever you like from the kitchen."

"Mmmm. Rashers of bacon, slabs of ham, wedges of hot apple pie," murmured Lucien. "Topped off with a hunk of Stilton."

"Savoring the thought of Stilton? Then it sounds as if you are well on the road to recovery, Mr. Harkness."

"Yes. Thanks to you." His fingers fumbled with the cuff of his nightshirt. "I cannot begin to tell you how grateful I am for all your kindness. Yet I'm sorry that you have been put to all the trouble of caring for me."

"You have nothing for which to be sorry."

He drew in a ragged breath. "Thank you for that as well. Your assurances were more balm for my spirit than I can say. I-I am not sure I could have lived with myself, thinking I had caused you such pain."

"Actually, it is we who should be begging your forgiveness. If I had been clearer in my description...if my sister had been a trifle less headstrong...and if Lord Killingworth had been a bit more circumspect in his anger, this attack on you might have been prevented."

"I doubt it." Lucien pulled a face. "If this dastard had planned all along to use me as a means of getting at Uncle Marcus, he would have found some other way to manage it." There was a pause as he watched Meredith lay the book aside and reach for the tray of medicines. "And as for your sister, she can hardly be blamed for reacting as she did."

"Perhaps not." Meredith took her time in measuring out a mixture. "Still, Eliza tends to have a bit of a temper."

That prompted a wry chuckle. "So I have noticed. But no more than Uncle Marcus." The twitch of his mouth stilled. "I must say, their first meeting was rather like seeing flint and steel rub together, wasn't it? I hope the sparks are not flying too thick downstairs."

"The atmosphere is not quite as hot as one might expect. They seem to have come to some sort of...agreement. At least, that is how it appears." She handed him the draught. "In any case, both of them have been rather too busy to quarrel of late. The earl has been holed up in his library, while my sister has occupied herself with poring over a mountain of papers and ledgers.”

Her lips crooked in a fond smile. “Eliza has a very good head for practical matters. She is extremely clever with numbers and analyzing expenses and that sort of thing.”

“Well, Uncle Marcus is most definitely not.” Realizing that his comment might sound a trifle disloyal, Lucien quickly added, “That is by his own admission, in case you are wondering.”

He paused for a moment. “Yet he is much more learned than most people realize. His knowledge of literature and history is really quite impressive. However, when it comes to mathematics and logistics of the actual running of his estate, he claims he is overmatched. Indeed, judging by all the curses and grimaces that accompany an attempt at balancing the accounts, one would think he was fighting the Battle of Badajoz single-handedly.”

“He is not alone,” said Meredith. “A number of the local gentlemen come to Eliza for her advice on business. Though, I might add, they are loath to admit it.”

Lucien looked thoughtful. “Your sister sounds quite remark-able. I wish I might have a chance to further the acquaintance. But it’s clear she wants nothing to do with me.”

“Eliza can be quick to anger and quick to leap into action, but she is also quick to admit when she is wrong.”

* * *

Had she made the right decision?

Eliza shoved the last of the books into her reticule, somehow managing to twist the cords into knots. No doubt they would prove difficult to undo once she returned to Killingworth Manor.

But no more so than her own tangled thoughts.

She could not keep the question from echoing once again in her head. Had she made the right decision in joining forces with the earl? Until lately, she had considered herself quite adept at summing up a situation and arriving at the correct course of action. But now, a nagging little inner voice was reminding her that she had been rather precipitous in her calculations, coming up with the wrong answer in regard to young Mr. Harkness.

And, if truth be told, in regard to Lord Killingworth as well.

Neither man was the beast she had thought him to be.

In the case of the earl, her tally on him had been off on a number of accounts. To begin with, she had thought that a rake-hell would lack any vestige of honor. Yet, whether she agreed with it or not, his demand that his nephew offer marriage to Meredith was motivated by commitment to a strict code of honor.

She had also imagined him to be a shallow, stupid man, interested only in pursuits of the flesh. His intellect, however, had proven to be surprisingly sharp. Not only was he well-read and insightful, but he also appeared willing—even eager—to expand the boundaries of his knowledge. How else to explain his determination to learn the running of his estate, no matter that it meant the hiring a female to teach him?

Oh, to be sure he had his faults. Probably quite a few. But in her first attempt at adding up the pluses and minuses of his character, Eliza had to admit she had gotten the equation all wrong.

And so she asked herself again—was she making another mistake this time?

Eliza bit her lip as she took a long moment to survey her snug study, with its familiar faded chintzes, well-worn books and waxed pine. Had Ned's comment contained more truth than she wished to acknowledge? Was she allowing herself to be seduced by the earl? Not physically, of course, but by the chance to expand her own little world, to take on the sort of challenge she had always dreamed about.

An exasperated sigh stole forth. She made precious few errors when it came to dealing with numbers. If only the same could be said for her dealings with people.

Her gaze lingered on a basket of dried herbs. She stood for

several moments, breathing in the subtle scents of lavender, thyme, and chamomile, and felt the scrunch of her features begin to ease somewhat. Despite her youth and lack of worldly experience, Meredith was not only a skilled healer, but also an excellent judge of people. And not only was her sister unintimidated by the Earl of Killingworth's growls and snarls, for some odd reason, she actually seemed to like him.

Eliza wasn't quite sure why.

But still, such a realization helped banish her misgivings, at least for the moment.

After adding a roll of pamphlets to the pocket of her pelisse, she reordered the stacks of books on her desk before quitting the cottage and set off at a brisk pace for Killingworth Manor. The die was cast, she told herself, wryly choosing an analogy in keeping with one of the earl's favorite pastimes. If it was a losing proposition, she could always gather up her vowels and leave the table.

In the meantime, she meant to profit from both the salary and the experience the earl was offering. And trifling annoyances such as lordly sarcasm or teasing would not deter her from her goal. She would do whatever it took to get the job done.

She would be tough. She would be patient. She would be hard-working. She would be innovative...

Hell's Bells.

She would even try to be nice to the dratted man, if that was what was necessary.

Eleven

"Rethatch Wicker's cottage...a dozen ewes to be added to the north meadows...switch from mangelwurzel to..." muttered the earl, his writing reduced to a hurried scrawl as he tried to keep pace with Eliza's orders.

"And if you and your new steward are riding out in the direction of the mill, ask Mr. Fleming if the new stone has arrived," finished Eliza. "That is, if Mr. Whitney has no objection to my suggestions."

Marcus laid aside his pen. "Sarcasm is not necessary to remind me of how little you like the arrangement, Miss Kirtland—there is precious little chance I shall ever forget it." On seeing the jut of her chin, he had to repress a smile. "However, even you have to admit that things are progressing rather well."

"Hmmph." With an exaggerated shrug, she went back to consulting her notes. "The young man does not appear unwilling to listen," she allowed. "Nor does he seem adverse to hard work."

Young man? He coughed to hide a chuckle. The fellow was at least a half dozen years her senior. "Well, he does come highly recommended."

"Ha, but by whom?" she said under her breath. Shuffling the

pages, she added in a louder voice, "It is too early to judge, sir. But I suppose I could be saddled with worse."

High praise indeed, thought the earl. He should hope so, given the amount of effort it had taken to search out the right man for the job. Not only was the candidate required to be diligent, trustworthy, and sharp-witted, but also liberal-minded enough to agree to some radical management notions—including a female as his nominal boss.

The earl's inquiries had turned up the name of Jock Whitney, whose father had worked for decades as the bailiff of a vast estate near Exeter. Having served a lengthy apprenticeship under his parent, the younger Whitney was eager for a chance to strike out on his own. Enough so that he was willing to agree to the rather peculiar terms of the contract.

To his credit, the fellow had not sought to change the conditions once he had been hired. There were, mused Marcus, all manner of subtle ways in which a new steward might have tried to discredit Miss Kirtland. Instead, he seemed to hold her and her ideas in genuine regard.

In turn, the young lady's barbs were becoming less and less pointed, as reflected by her last comment.

"Speaking of Whitney," continued the earl when she finally looked up. "He wished me to ask whether you thought the acreage near the millpond might be better used for millet rather than rye."

"An interesting question." Eliza began to chew on the end of her pen. "I suppose he has read Remington's essay on soil nutrients."

"Possibly," murmured the earl, hoping she wouldn't inquire whether he had done the same. He had been burning the candles into the wee hours of the night studying sheep and cows, but he drew the line at dirt.

"I shall have to think on it for a day." Turning from the table she had commandeered as her work space, she moved to the windows. "Why is he not here? There are a number of other matters I should have liked to discuss in person."

"A section of fencing by the cliffs was washed out by last night's heavy rain. He wished to oversee the repairs himself, to make sure they were done right."

"Hmmph." A nod, however, indicated her grudging approval. "In that case, they, too, can wait until the morrow." Eliza's gaze lingered a bit longer on the distant pastureland, as if her thoughts had momentarily wandered far afield. Then, gathering the ends of her shawl, she stepped back from the leaded panes.

"During my afternoon walk, I shall try to pass by the milking barns and see how work is going on the new churns." The fringe was slowly unraveling in her fingers. "Of course, if I have any suggestions, I shall make note of them and let Mr. Whitney know later."

Marcus felt a sudden twinge of sympathy. Her sense of frustration was entirely understandable. The ideas, the innovations were hers, and yet she must cloak her intellect in the same drab cloth that hid her physical attributes.

"The barns can also wait until tomorrow," he murmured. "Why not ride out with us this afternoon. We'll make a thorough tour of the south end of the manor, to make sure you are satisfied with the way your plans are being implemented."

Her eyes narrowed, though not enough to hide the spark of excitement that set their emerald color aglitter. "I—I thought you said my role in running Killingworth Manor must remain a secret."

"I did. And it must. But as long as you are a guest under my roof, it will not draw undue attention if you accompany me on a leisurely ride. Nor will it seem odd if my steward joins us for part of the time."

She hesitated, pride warring with a burning curiosity to see how things were progressing.

"Ah, well. If you would rather not..."

"I shall be ready in ten minutes."

Five was more like it, thought the earl with an inward grin on watching her hurry toward the stables. As she drew nearer, his amusement faded. He could see she had not changed her garments, save for replacing the shawl with a short spenser jacket and adding an unattractive bonnet. That she didn't appear to possess a riding habit made him question for a moment whether his suggestion had been a wise one. It hadn't occurred to him that she might not know how to ride and so he had chosen a rather spirited filly for her mount.

The problem was, given her present prickly mood, it was highly unlikely she would admit to not knowing how to handle the reins, no matter if she had never been in the saddle before. He could only hope that she wouldn't take a bad tumble.

His misgivings were quickly dispelled as the groom helped her up and adjusted the reins. Despite her billowing skirts, she had a firm seat and a calm authority that stilled the filly's nervous prancing. And, he added to himself, a nicely turned ankle and calf, which the breeze was now exposing with gratifying regularity.

As if sensing the drift of his thoughts, Eliza urged her mount into a brisk trot. "Where to first?" she demanded over her shoulder.

A light touch of his heels brought his stallion abreast of her. "I thought you might like to see how work is progressing on the mill pond before we meet up with Whitney."

Her only response was a curt nod. They rode on in silence until the way led into a grove of beech and live oaks, slowing their pace to a walk.

Seeing a frown start to form, Marcus sought to allay her impatience. "We needn't rush, Miss Kirtland. If we can't cover all the ground today, there is always tomorrow."

"Perhaps there is tomorrow, but I shall not be a guest for much longer," she muttered. "So I must try to accomplish as much as I can before it's time to take our leave from here."

He mulled over the import of her words before replying. "Yes, thanks to your sister and you, Lucien is well on the mend. I believe that only this morning, he managed a short walk through the garden." With Meredith steadying the young man's steps, he might add. Though he didn't.

"It is Meredith who should receive all the thanks. I deserve little credit—you know well enough that my first inclination was not that of the Good Samaritan."

"Yet you allowed your sister to convince you otherwise."

"So I did."

He thought he detected a flicker of emotion shade her profile. Curious, he pressed on. "Have you any regrets?"

"In retrospect, that would be a churlish sentiment to admit to."

The answer was oblique at best, but he let it pass. Their horses splashed through a shallow stream, then climbed a short rise into open meadow. Marcus, too, made a slight change in direction. "They seem to have developed a certain...friendship, despite the rocky beginning."

"Unlike their relatives." The filly gave a wicker and tossed her head, causing Eliza to relax her grip on the reins. Perhaps realizing her tone had grown just as tight, she let out a deep breath and added, "Yes, they appear to enjoy each other's company."

"Unlike their relatives," echoed the earl, though he said it with a great deal more humor than she had.

"This is a business arrangement, Lord Killingworth," she replied. "Whether we like or dislike each other is not part of the equation."

Damnation. Why did she insist on being as stiff and dry as one of the numbers in his ledgers? He knew she had a keen sense of humor, though she took pains to keep it as well-shrouded as the curves of her bosom.

Grimacing in exasperation, he couldn't refrain from answering her snap for snap. "Ah. I shall make a note of it in my copybook. Lesson number one for Wednesday—the duties of a steward include rebuffing any attempt at polite conversation with gratuitous rudeness."

His words seemed to take her by surprise. Her brow furrowed and there was an awkward pause before she replied. "I—I was not intending to be deliberately rude, sir. Merely...businesslike."

"You might want to make a few notes of your own, Miss Kirtland. When I do business with someone, I prefer it to be a pleasant exchange. That way I am more likely to want to repeat the experience. I imagine most people feel the same way." He slanted a sideways glance at her, interested to catch her reaction.

There was a pronounced scowl, then the scrunch of her lips gave an odd little tweak. "I shall make a note of it in my workbook. Lesson number two for Wednesday—the duties of a steward include humoring one's employer."

Though her expression was not quite a smile, it was getting close. "I would offer to sing, or to dance atop the saddle, but as I do both very badly, it would definitely not be a pleasant experience."

Marcus gave an inward grin, delighted he had unwound at least one layer of her protective covering. "I shall settle for polite conversation."

"Very well." Eliza shifted in her saddle. "What do you wish to discuss, sir?"

"We were speaking of your sister and my nephew. I was curious as to whether you were still dead set against the acquaintance, given your initial opinion of the young man?"

"My initial opinion was wrong," she conceded with hesitation. "Mr. Harkness seems a...decent young man."

His brow waggled. "Miss Kirtland in error? Did I hear correctly?"

"I can be wrong on occasion." Two bright spots of color had appeared on her cheeks, whether from the wind or some other cause was impossible to tell. "Though not often."

Marcus couldn't help but chuckle.

"Fie on you sir! Overt mockery is hardly polite." She was, however, still sporting the odd half smile.

"Ah, but there is a difference between teasing and mocking. Teasing is a more—"

A loud hail from up ahead interrupted his words. He looked around, surprised that he hadn't noticed the rocky cliffs or the sound of the surf until that moment.

"Lord Killingworth." Whitney sounded a bit winded as he jogged over to greet them. And well he might. Despite the stiff breeze, he was stripped to his shirtsleeves and the mud on his person made it clear he had been doing more than just issuing orders.

"The job is nearly done, sir. Another hour or two and there will be no further danger of sheep straying over the edge." He gestured at the sturdy posts and heavy rails that guarded the crumbling rock. "Though it took a bit longer, I had the holes dug a foot deeper and packed with crushed stone. That way, the fence may weather the elements with less danger of collapse. I hope that meets with your approval."

Eliza gave an almost imperceptible nod.

"Yes. Good thinking," said the earl as he surveyed the expanse of work. In doing so, his eye caught on a small area near where the rails took a turn inland. "While you are here, should not that bit of overhanging ledge be chipped away? It looks as if one good storm would knock it loose and cause a good deal of damage."

Both Whitney and Eliza looked to where he had indicated. "Aye, milord. You're right," exclaimed the steward. "I'll see to it directly."

"I think the men can finish up on their own," said Marcus, feeling oddly gratified by his contribution to the efforts. Perhaps there was hope that he could be a competent master of his lands.

"I'd rather you accompany us on a tour of the south fields. I may have some suggestions to make, once we see for ourselves how all the work is progressing."

Whitney's gaze made only the slightest flicker in Eliza's direction. "An excellent idea, sir. "I'll just be a moment."

As the two of them waited for him to fetch his coat and horse, the earl heard a murmur mix in with the gusting breeze.

"Lesson number three for Wednesday—the duties of a steward include acknowledging when one's employer shows a marked improvement in his attention to detail."

* * *

THE EARL WAS IMPROVING IN HIS GRASP OF ESTATE management, Eliza admitted to herself later that afternoon. In leaps and bounds. Her eyes scanned down the ruled page, checking over the past month's expenditures. Why, he had even made some headway in getting the numbers to add up as they should. She made several minor corrections, then let the ledger fall closed.

Would that she could figure out the sum of Lord Killingworth with half as much accuracy.

Thinking his demand that she teach him how to run the Manor was made out of whimsy or boredom, she had been determined to test his mettle. Indeed, the lengthy list of things to do might have intimidated even the most dedicated of pupils. There were dreadfully dull technical treatises on agriculture and animal husbandry to read, practical lectures to assimilate and hands-on inspections to make, not to speak of getting to know his tenants.

If truth be told, Eliza hadn't expected him to stick it out a week.

She let out a harried sigh. Well, not only had the earl stuck it out, he had proven to be an extremely quick study. Unlike many people, he listened well, and when he understood a fundamental concept, he asked intelligent questions to further his understanding of a subject. The afternoon ride had shown he was observant to boot. His suggestion about the ledge had been only one of several excellent recommendations.

In short, the Earl of Killingworth had shown himself to be smart, diligent, thoughtful, and determined.

And amusing.

Loath as she was to acknowledge it, she had enjoyed their lively bantering. His teasing lit a certain spark in her that was far more complex than mere anger. It was odd how she had, on first impression, thought him a cold, hard gentleman—*Chilling*worth had seemed a more apt moniker than his true name. Now, it was difficult to imagine she had missed such nuances as the subtle shades of intelligence in his amber eyes, or the rich depth of his laughter, or—

Eliza stopped herself with a rueful grimace. Hell's Bells, she was in danger of sounding like a besotted schoolgirl. It would not do to forget that he was also a practiced charmer, a man who made a habit of seducing women, drinking to excess, frequenting the gaming hells and...engaging in vices she probably couldn't begin to name.

Or imagine.

Besides, it wasn't as if he was waxing poetic about her.

The earl thought her rude. She brushed an errant curl from her cheek. And what of his snide remark concerning hairpins? Her hand came up to fiddle with the tightly wound bun at her neck. He had implied she was rigid, unbending, incapable of having fun.

It was, she thought with a slight sniff, a rather unfair—not to speak of unflattering—assessment. With a sick mother, a younger sister, and a dwindling nest egg, she had had little opportunity to think of serendipitous pleasures.

Cupping her chin, Eliza contemplated the drops of rain that were beginning to spatter against the windowpanes. A sudden squall had blown in from the sea, bringing with it a thick mist that had turned the sky a dull pewter and obscured all but the closest trees. As she watched the landscape dissolve into naught but an amorphous blur, she couldn't help thinking how strange it was that things could look so sparkling clear one moment and so fuzzy the next.

"Am I interrupting your work?"

Eliza turned with a start, then smiled. "No. Just woolgathering, I'm afraid." She hastily opened one of the journals at her elbow. "However, I really should not be wasting my time in idleness. I have a good deal of reading to plough through."

Her sister's brow creased as she took a seat near the desk. "Don't apologize. You should do it more often—woolgathering, that is, not analyzing the latest mechanical devices for cutting a furrow through the earth."

Meredith smoothed at the sash of her dress before continuing. "I fear you are pushing yourself too hard, especially of late. It wouldn't hurt to lay aside the books and spend a few hours doing...nothing."

The journal fell back on the pile with a thump. "You, too?" muttered Eliza through clenched teeth. Before her sister could respond, she shifted uncomfortably in her chair and went on. "You think I should...let my hair down, is that it?"

Meredith smiled. "I suppose that is one way of putting it."

"Hmmph. Well, I'd rather you didn't." In the ensuing silence, her fingers unconsciously strayed to the nape of her neck. "Do you find me too stiff? Too serious?"

"Good Heavens, that's not at all what I meant." Meredith's reply was said gently, but the gaze that she fixed on Eliza's taut features was a good deal more probing. "I spoke out of concern, not criticism. At times, I worry that you are taking on too many responsibilities."

"I like keeping busy," she said, a note of defensiveness creeping into her voice.

Her sister looked from Eliza's shadowed profile to the heavy ledgers to the open inkwell. "Is there some particular reason you are working yourself to the bone? I thought you had finished preparing the estimates for Mr. Hardy's alehouse."

"I have." Eliza's mouth quirked. For reasons she could not quite explain, even to herself, she had held off in telling her sister about the arrangement with the earl. It would, she knew, have to come out at some point, so she decided it might as well be now. "But I have a new client."

As expected, the announcement caused a ripple of surprise in Meredith's eyes. "A new client? Given all the recent events, I can't for the life of me imagine when you had time to arrange that. Who is it?"

"The Earl of Killingworth."

* * *

THE EARL STRETCHED HIS LEGS OUT TOWARD THE FIRE and tried to concentrate on the printed page. Yet try as he might to visualize the alignment of pulleys and levers described in the paragraph, all he could picture in his mind was a pair of exotic green eyes, a tigerish scowl, a...

With a snort of exasperation, he tossed the book aside. Why was he was bedeviled by thoughts of Miss Kirtland when he had a good deal of other, more important, matters to occupy his attention? If he thought of her at all, it should only be in the context of their business arrangement—say, for example, to review one of her myriad lectures on estate management. But somehow, contemplating an explanation of crop rotation or tilling methods was not nearly so intriguing as picturing the defiant tilt of her chin, or the way her unruly wheaten curls refused to be tamed by a regiment of hairpins.

Bloody hell. It wasn't as if she thought of him. Except, perhaps, for the few seconds it took to consign him to whatever circle of the Inferno that Dante had reserved for dissolute scoundrels.

Muttering an oath, he rose and poured himself a generous splash of brandy. It went down in one hurried gulp, no matter that the fiery spirits left his throat feeling a bit scalded.

The sensation was rather like an encounter with the young lady herself—a complex mixture of spice, sweetness, and heat that was not altogether pleasant at first, but left one wanting another taste.

After refilling his glass, the earl moved to stand before the blazing logs. Why he should savor the idea of their working together was puzzling in the extreme. She was all business, while he preferred his females to be all pleasure. No matter how he looked at the problem, it simply didn't add up.

But then, he had much to learn before he would be proficient in mathematics.

Twelve

The stallion's frightened whinny was nearly drowned out by the crackling flames. Smoke was fast enveloping the stall, thick with wisps of blackened hay. It took only a few minutes for the fire to spread to the adjoining enclosure, setting alight an old carriage harness hung out for repairs. The tangle of burning leather quickly snapped and shattered a lantern.

Glass exploded, spilling oil onto a pile of rags. Sparks lit the soaked fabric and suddenly flames were shooting up to the rafters.

Panicked, the big animal reared up again and again, hooves splintering the singed wood as it desperately sought escape from the growing inferno. The noise finally roused a young stableboy who was sleeping above the tack room. He stumbled down the stairs, finally awaking to the danger below.

Shielding his face, the lad tried to make his way to the stall, but the heat and smoke forced him back. Another snort of terror from the thrashing stallion drove him to try again. Dropping to the stone floor, he managed to crawl half the distance before a falling timber caught him a glancing blow on the shoulder.

He tried to cry out, but the sound was hardly more than a choked sob. The air was acrid and billowing clouds dark as slate...

"Bloody Hell!" Blinded by the swirling smoke, the earl needed several precious minutes to locate the unconscious lad and drag him to safety.

It was a damn lucky thing, thought Marcus, that he had been unable to fall asleep earlier in the evening. Rather than lie awake counting sheep, he had gone down to his study with the intent of finishing the accounting for the millpond project. From the windows opposite his desk, he had noticed the faint orange glow and had lost no time in racing down the graveled path.

"Come, Jem, take a breath!" he ordered, thumping some air into the frightened lad's lungs. "You must run to the house and wake the others." Without waiting for a reply, the earl turned, ready to plunge back into the roaring blaze.

"Milord!"

"Whitney!" he answered. "Ring the alarm. Open the rest of these stalls, then gather what help you can and see if you can prevent the fire from spreading to the other wing."

"But sir—"

Marcus had already disappeared into the spark and flames.

* * *

"More water there!" Whitney paused long enough in his labors at the well to point to a smoking beam. The buckets passed hand to hand down the line of servants, and the threat was quickly extinguished.

Wiping the sweat from his brow, he yielded his place to a fresh man and went to inspect the damage. Smoke still wafted up from charred wood, puddles sloshed underfoot and an eerie hissing stirred through the wet embers, but by some miracle the fire had been contained to one small wing of the massive stables.

"Is everyone accounted for?" demanded the steward, as he peered into the rubble.

"Aye, Mr. Whitney. And it appears all the animals be safe as well," answered the grizzled gamekeeper, who had been one of the first to arrive on the scene.

"Well done," he sighed, directing a nod of thanks to the exhausted group of servants and nearby tenants who had answered the alarm bell. His look of relief suddenly faded to one of distress. "His Lordship—Dear God, has anyone seen the earl?"

There was a dead silence before one of the women pointed to a mass of fallen timbers blocking the way to the hayloft. "He 'eard a noise, and went back. Up there."

"The devil take it." Whitney grabbed an axe, but before he could begin cutting through the rubble, a shape appeared from the darkness.

Marcus resembled nothing so much as his namesake—two glittering feline eyes peered out from a face near black as midnight from its coating of soot. As his shirt was in tatters, the rest of his flesh was in a similar state. Whitney blinked in disbelief, but the sigh—and soft mewing emanating from the vicinity of the earl's chest—was no figments of his imagination.

Cradled in Marcus's arms were three tiny kittens, woefully bedraggled and covered in ash, but otherwise unharmed.

"Here, let me take them, sir." Eliza shouldered past the astonished steward and reached for the balls of fluff.

The earl stared at her chafed palms, rubbed raw from helping with the buckets of water. "Hell's teeth, Miss Kirtland, go back to the house and have your sister attend to those injuries," he growled. "Have you no more sense than to risk life and limb out here?"

"Apparently no more sense than you," she replied, removing the kittens from his grasp. She passed them on to a fumbling Whitney, then took firm hold of Marcus's wrist. "Come with me. It is you who need medical attention. Those look to be some rather nasty scrapes and burns on your arms."

"Mere scratches," he grumbled. Though he fully intended to

take her to task for such high-handed measures, he suddenly felt rather unsteady on his feet. "No reason to fuss over them."

Paying no attention to his protest, Eliza tightened her grip and marched off. Too exhausted to put up further resistance, the earl allowed himself to be led outside, to a spot by the paddock where Meredith was already treating several of the farmers for minor injuries.

"Sit here," ordered Eliza, forcing him down on a bale of hay. "And don't move." She was back in a moment with a bowl of hot water, a crock of ointment and a length of linen bandage.

"Just what do you intend to do with those?" he asked, giving the items a dubious look.

"I should think it would be obvious."

"But—" The sponge touched his shoulders. "OUCH!"

"Do stop yowling. That can't possibly hurt."

"Miss Kirtland, I—"

It was now her hands upon his bare flesh, massaging the fragrant balm into the scraped and knotted muscles. Feeling for some unaccountable reason as if the cat had got his tongue, Marcus fell silent as her touch glided down the curve of his biceps.

"You what?" she asked softly.

"I—that is, if I had wished to be smacked and pummeled to death, I would have stayed among the falling timbers."

There was a ripping sound as Eliza readied a length of linen. "Speaking of which, what possessed you to go into the blaze alone? You should have waited for help before doing anything so foolhardy."

Marcus gave what was meant as an indifferent shrug, though it ended in a wince as she tied off the bandage with a sharp tug.

She matched his show of nonchalance. "Well, I feel I must warn you, sir—as soon as word spreads of what happened tonight, you may be in danger of losing your reputation."

His head jerked up, the devil-may-care expression slipping

from his features. "What in the name of Lucifer is that supposed to mean?

"The Black Cat..." She paused to tear off another piece of cloth.

"Confound it, Miss Kirtland! If you are going to suggest that I was in any way responsible for—"

"...and his kittens." Eliza shook her head in mock dismay. "Really, sir, it is going to be rather difficult to maintain the image of a cold, ruthless predator if you insist on doing things like risking your own skin to rescue helpless animals."

"Er...ah," He gave a gruff cough. "I wasn't thinking very clearly."

An exaggerated arch of her brow was her only reply. Eliza worked on in silence for a few minutes longer before knotting off the last bandage.

"There." She leaned back and dusted her hands. "That should do it." From somewhere in the shadows she produced a blanket and draped it over his shoulders. "Now, you had better return to the Manor and get some hot tea and some sleep."

"Not at all tired. Don't need any rest," he muttered. "Need to help Whitney." Unfortunately the assertion was belied by the fact that he nearly fell flat on his face on trying to rise.

"Mr. Whitney and the men have things well under control. There's little more to be done, save for settling the horses and putting out the few remaining pockets of embers."

"But—"

"Enough heroics for one night, Lord Killingworth," she said firmly, her hand steadying his swaying step. "Stop arguing and let us be off."

Heroics?

Suddenly speechless, Marcus abandoned any thoughts of further protest and followed meekly at her side.

* * *

"Rags and oil, you say?"

"Yes, milord. I took it upon myself to make a thorough inspection at first light. There are signs of a forced latch on the tack room door, and the remnants of oil-soaked rags are still lying about." He crossed his arms. "And Jem found signs of footprints in the stand of beech nearby. There is no question in my mind—the fire was deliberately set."

Marcus flexed his scraped knuckles and turned to stare at the glowing hearth.

From her seat near the fire, Eliza was unable to read his expression. "It would seem that someone is hellbent on seeing you driven out of the area, sir," she murmured. "Have you any idea who it might be?"

He looked back and slowly shook his head.

"No enemies you can think of?" she persisted.

His lips curved into a sardonic smile. "I can think of a good many I have made over the years, Miss Kirtland. But they are all in London, not here in South Dorset Downs."

"On the contrary, Lord Killingworth. I think it quite likely that at least one of them has strayed from Town."

"It could be that someone had a grudge against one of the grooms. Or was simply bent on mischief—"

Her derisive snort cut him off. "Fustian, sir! Given the other incidents, there isn't a snowball's chance in Hell that this latest attack is mere coincidence."

Whitney cleared his throat. "Er, I would have to agree with Miss Kirtland's assessment, sir." Though clearly uncomfortable raising the subject, he nonetheless went on. "I know of what happened to Mr. Harkness. And I have heard the recent rumors regarding...other attacks, sir. There is no denying something havey-cavey is afoot here."

"But why?" The earl appeared to be speaking more to himself than the others. "There was certainly ample opportunity for foul play in London. Why wait until now to—"

His musings were cut off by a sharp knock on the door. Before he could respond, it flew open and his nephew hobbled in, closely attended by Meredith. Taking in the pallor of the young man's features and the hobbling shuffle of his movements, Marcus quirked a grimace, first at Lucien, then his companion. "I wonder that you have been allowed to leave your bed and exert yourself in such a manner. It does not seem wise."

"To the devil with my bed. If you are to have a council of war, Uncle Marcus, I wish to be a part of it."

"It is merely a—"

Lucien's jaw tightened. "Don't fob me off as if I were naught but a grubby schoolboy, sir. Despite what you think, I'm not a complete idiot. Nor a sniveling coward."

"I think you neither, Lucien, but—"

"Then no 'buts' about it," replied his nephew.

"But..." Sunk by his own logic, the earl cast a baleful look at the others, as if fishing for some help.

"Perhaps I may even surprise you and have a useful idea or two," added Lucien with a self-deprecating shrug.

Inwardly applauding the young man's show of spirit, Eliza hid a smile by regarding the tips of her slippers. It was obvious the earl was unaccustomed to having his wishes opposed, especially when he employed that tone of voice. Whitney, too, seemed to be finding the situation diverting. To cover a twitch of amusement, his gaze was now riveted on the ceiling molding.

Seeing he could expect no show of support from either of his advisors, Marcus threw up his hands in surrender. "Very well. I suppose you might as well take a seat."

Meredith moved quickly, choosing to interpret the grudging invitation as including her as well.

"By all means, you too," grumbled the earl. "Shall I ring for tea and make it a proper social gathering?"

"Perhaps refreshments would not be a bad idea, as someone appears to be rather peckish this morning," replied Eliza. Ignoring the earl's dark look, she opened a small notebook and turned to a fresh page. "In any case, Mr. Harkness is quite right. The more minds that are put to the task, the quicker we will be able to figure out what is going on here."

"Hmmph." Marcus did, however, refrain from further sarcasm.

"Mr. Whitney was just informing us of his early morning investigations," explained Eliza, and then proceeded to recount the steward's discoveries.

"As you can see, the evidence all indicates it was arson rather than accident. Hardly a surprise, I might add, unless one is a greater believer in coincidence than I am." Taking the ensuing bit of silence as encouragement to go on, Eliza tapped her pen against the blank paper. "The question we were just beginning to address is, why does someone seem intent on ruining the earl—either in name or in fact?"

"Some sort of personal grudge?" ventured Meredith.

"A, er, significant monetary loss at the gaming tables?" murmured Lucien.

All eyes turned toward Marcus. "Both are possible," he conceded. "Though not from the recent past. So it strikes me as peculiar that my unknown adversary would choose here and now. Or that he would pick Lucien as one of his targets. Anyone who knows me must be aware that the two of us have never had a particularly...cordial relationship."

"An eye for an eye—revenge has been a powerful motive since Biblical days," murmured Whitney. "Is there some individual who might feel compelled to avenge a...physical injury, whether to himself or someone close to him?" The words were chosen with care, but it was clear that the steward had heard rumors of the earl's involvement in several duels. "That may explain such a violent attack on a family member."

The earl leaned back in his chair. "Though you are all much too polite to be so blunt, what you really mean to ask is what sort of acts on my part could provoke such animosity? Have I bedded another man's wife? Have I been lucky enough at cards to leave another man's fortune and future in ruin? Have I left another man lying in his own blood on the dueling grounds?"

Beneath the thin veneer of cynicism was the note of another, much deeper layer of emotion. As Eliza watched the play of shadows flicker over his face, she couldn't help but wonder at the stark contrasts it presented. *Light and dark.* And yet nothing about the earl was black and white, she decided, but rather infinite shades of gray.

"The answer is yes," continued Marcus. "To all of the above."

A log snapped in the fire, sending up a crackle of sparks.

"You are painting a blacker picture of yourself than is fair, sir," protested Lucien with some heat of his own.

"Am I?"

"Yes. The incidents you describe are..." The young man shot an apologetic look at the two ladies. "...unfortunately part of accepted behavior within the highest circles of the *ton*. You are no less honorable than most titled gentlemen in living by Society's rules. Indeed, you are better than most. Your integrity is unquestioned—why, even those who do not like you admit you are a man of principle. There has never been so much as a whisper to imply that any of your successes were achieved by underhanded methods, so do not speak as if you have committed some smarmy deed, deserving of retribution." Lucien drew in a deep breath. "I know you have not."

A look of genuine surprise ghosted across the earl's features on hearing his nephew's impassioned defense of his character. It was gone in an instant, replaced by his more usual expression of sardonic bemusement. "I would have expected you to be among the most vocal in condemning me as harsh and unfair."

"As I said, Uncle Marcus, perhaps there are a number of things about me that you will find unexpected."

* * *

THERE WAS A LENGTHY SILENCE AS THE EARL ROSE AND added another log to the fire. Turning abruptly from the flare of the flames, he addressed the others. "Judge me as you will, my only real concern is my unknown adversary. It appears he will stop at nothing to ruin me, no matter how many innocent people he harms in the process. I mean, of course, to hunt him down. But it may prove dangerous to anyone associated with me. You have all seen the violence of which he is capable."

His brows drew together, putting Eliza in mind of a hawk homing in on its prey. He then straightened and squared his broad shoulders, only heightening the predatory image. If she were wont to wagering, she decided, her money would certainly not be bet against the earl when he came face to face with his enemy.

His hooded eyes, now nearly dark as midnight, turned to fix on Whitney. "Perhaps you wish to reconsider your employment, as the terms of the contract appear to have changed. I would understand it if you choose to return to Exeter, at least until this is over."

The young man did not twitch a hair under the intense scrutiny. "We have already put a great deal of work into Killingworth Manor, milord. If you don't mind, I would prefer to stay and fight to make sure it has not been all for naught."

A glimmer of approval lightened the earl's brooding countenance. He gave a curt nod. "Thank you, Whitney. No doubt we will have our work cut out for us. But the sooner we put an end to this nasty business, the better for everyone."

Eliza was not surprised by the young man's decision. She had, over the past fortnight, been favorably impressed with his demeanor. Quick-witted and tough-minded, he would prove a valuable ally in hunting down their adversary.

"To begin with," continued Marcus. "I shall have you removed without delay to London, Lucien, where you should be safe from further attack. And the Kirtlands will leave immediately for—"

There was a bark of outrage from his nephew. "My limp has done nothing to slow my wits, Uncle Marcus. I'll not be packed off like a helpless fema—" He bit off the last word and glanced in embarrassment at the two sisters. "Er, that is, like a helpless fool. I'm not going anywhere and that's flat."

"Count me in as well, sir," said Meredith, her resolve evident despite the softness of her voice. "I may not be able to throw a punch or fire a pistol, but I know there must be some way I can help."

"Miss Kirtland!" The bellow was somewhere between an accusation and an appeal. "Can't you drum some sense into these young people?"

"They seem perfectly sensible to me, sir," replied Eliza calmly.

His jaw dropped. "Surely you don't mean to suggest—"

"Suggest that they are right in demanding to be part of the action?" Her pen moved over the page of her notebook as if jotting down some relevant point. In truth, she was doodling a sketch. Of a very large and very angry cat, ears flattened, claws bared.

After a quick glance up, she added a set of fangs.

"Yes, of course I am. You don't actually think that I am going anywhere either, do you? We have a contract, Lord Killingworth, and I mean to hold you to it."

He frowned slightly. "If it is a matter of salary, Miss Kirtland, be assured you will receive what I—"

"It's not about money, sir. It's about principle." Forestalling the reply she saw forming on his lips, she quickly added, "I dislike being threatened or bullied. And I have as strong a grudge against this dastard as you do."

The earl's fingers drummed upon the mantel. "Will no one in this room show any common sense?"

Silence answered the appeal.

"Hmmph."

Eliza sensed that the slowing beat signaled surrender.

"Oh very well," he muttered. "Seeing we are to join forces, I think it is high time for us to go on the offensive against our enemy, rather than sit back and let him make another attack."

"Right you are, sir. As a first move, why don't Robbie and I make a few inquiries around the village," suggested Whitney. "The efforts and funds that you have ploughed into the Manor of late have yielded a change of heart in most of the local people. From what I gather, they would be sorry to see you pack up and leave. So let us see what information or leads we might uncover with a discreet question or two."

"Very discreet," cautioned Lucien. "Let us not tip our hand that we suspect a connection between all the various attacks. If we go about our usual routine, we have a better chance of luring him into making another move. And when he does, we shall be ready to spring a trap."

"That is a very sound strategy," allowed the earl.

"From an ancient Chinese philosopher whose work I read at Oxford, sir," murmured his nephew. "*The Art of War*."

Eliza observed the exchange of smiles between the two men with a curve of her own lips. She had a feeling that one of the alliances forged tonight would last far after the battle was over. For some reason, that pleased her.

"Do be careful, Mr. Whitney," added Meredith. "Whoever is responsible is extremely dangerous."

"Aye, miss." The steward smiled grimly as he turned to take his leave. "But if I were him, I'd be quaking in my boots at the prospect of having to face off against this little army."

They began to file out after him, the earl having dismissed them with a distracted nod. However, as Eliza gathered her papers and brought up the rear, he stopped her with a low murmur.

"Might I have a word, Miss Kirtland?"

"Yes. Of course." She wasn't quite sure what to expect. Up until recently, a stinging set-down for contradicting his wishes would have followed. Or simply an imperious order, issued with infuriating sarcasm. Yet of late, his moods had been far less predictable.

He took his time in speaking, giving Eliza an extra moment to study his profile. At first glance, the chiseled features were so harshly handsome that they appeared impervious to any self-doubt. But as he turned, she admitted that first impressions could be deceiving. Softened in morning sunlight, his face was far more nuanced than she had thought on first acquaintance. Tiny lines etched the corners of his eyes, the blades of his cheekbones were blunted by a shadow of regret, and the pinch of his mouth was anything but arrogant.

"You think it wise to involve the young people?" he asked slowly.

The weight of his words was a further surprise. Eliza realized just how much he felt that the burden of their safety was resting on his shoulders.

"You are asking for *my* advice?"

"Don't sound as if you are in need of smelling salts." The quip of sardonic humor was not quite as sharp as usual. "I defer to your superior wisdom on a great many subjects these days."

"Yes, but this is a far cry from deciding whether mangel wurtzels would yield more profits than alfalfa."

"And a good deal more costly if I err."

"You are worried—" began Eliza, only to have him cut her off.

"It may come as a shock to you, but I *do* have feelings. "Marcus raked a hand through his hair, unmindful of the curling tangle that fell over his collar.

"Other than lust, greed and vanity."

"I did not mean to disparage your feelings, sir."

"Just my character." He looked down at the carpet rather than at her. "You have reason to do so. I am not proud of my past."

The frank admission drew a rueful sigh from Eliza. "If we are to be brutally honest with each other, I'm not feeling very good about my own actions of late. The truth is, we all make mistakes."

"I doubt yours have had as grievous consequences as mine."

"Had I not judged you, or your nephew, so harshly, Lucien would not have suffered such horrible injuries," she replied. "I was so certain I was right that I mentioned my misgivings to my neighbor and, well...I have learned a lesson or two about my own overweening pride."

A spark seemed to light his gaze, yet it died so quickly she wondered if she had only imagined its fire.

"Ah, well, now that we have both admitted to being human, perhaps we ought to return to the question of our two young relatives," said Marcus gruffly. "I cannot like having them exposed to further risks."

"Nor can I," she replied. "But in this, I feel they have the right to make their own decision."

"You have a good deal of influence, though. They admire both your wisdom and your courage. If you were to counsel that discretion would be the better part of valor..."

Had she just heard a compliment, however oblique? Flustered, she caught only the last little bit of what he was saying. "What?"

"My aunt." He looked at her quizzically. "I do have a family—I did not emerge full grown from Minerva's forehead, you know. I was saying that I am sure I could convince her to invite the betrothed couple for a visit to London. It would all be very proper. Not to speak of very safe."

Before she could react, he added, "I would of course, wish for you to accompany them. Your well-being is of no less importance to me."

Eliza managed to swallow the odd little lump in her throat. "I thank you for your concern, milord. It would, no doubt, be the prudent course of action. But I cannot in good conscience leave you here to deal with the matter, just because things have taken a dangerous turn."

She lifted her chin. "A partnership is a partnership. I have not forgotten that against all common sense, you showed faith in me.

So, until we have caught the dastard, I'm afraid you are stuck with me."

"I can think of worse fates," he murmured.

"And I am sure I speak for Meredith and Lucien as well."

The earl tilted his head in what may—or may not—have been a nod. In any case he voiced no further objection.

Feeling slightly off balance, Eliza cleared her throat with a brusque cough. "Excellent. Then, assuming we understand each other, I believe I shall try to grab a bit of rest." Surveying his bandaged hands and scraped cheek, she added, "As should you, milord. Under the circumstances, I think we may postpone our daily review until the morrow."

Marcus lowered his lashes, making it impossible to see his eyes. A tiny spark seemed to glimmer through the dark fringe, though she couldn't tell whether it meant he was annoyed or amused.

"Yes, Miss Kirtland, I think we have an understanding."

Thirteen

"The barn," said Eliza as she scanned down her list at the following morning's meeting with the earl. Ever practical, she had not forgotten the responsibilities of the Manor. "We will have to budget in funds for its repair."

"Hmmm," was his noncommittal reply.

"It may mean we have to defer one of the other projects. I would suggest..." Seeing that Marcus appeared distracted, she stopped. "Perhaps we ought to discuss this another time."

"Hmmm."

The thump of the ledger falling shut finally got his attention.

"Sorry. Do go on."

"You may add another lesson to your copybook, sir," said Eliza. "Sometimes it is better to set work aside than go through the motions when your mind refuses to attend to the business at hand. That is how mistakes are made."

"Ah. I shall make a note of it—*Try like the devil to avoid errors of judgment.*" Marcus spoke with his usual dry detachment, but Eliza caught the bleakness of his expression as he slowly spun a pen upon the blotter. "Well, I have certainly been a dismal failure on that score."

Shocked by his tone, she laid her hand on his sleeve. "Lord Killingworth, you cannot blame yourself for another man's perfidy."

"No?" He rose abruptly and went to stand by the windows. "Your sister may have a forgiving heart, but from you I expect to hear naught but the harsh realities of the matter. You need not humor me."

Eliza refused to be brushed off so easily. Scraping back her chair, she went to join him. "When have you ever known me to humor you, sir?"

That softened his cynicism, but only for a moment. The glint of amusement quickly died away, leaving a dullness to his gaze.

Without thinking, she reached out to touch his cheek. His skin was still scraped but surprisingly warm. As her fingertips traced the line of his jaw, she was aware of the faint stubbling of whiskers.

He stiffened.

"I have none of Meredith's natural grace with people." She was close enough to breathe in the subtle scent of bay rum, with hints of an intriguing masculine spice she could not put a name to. "I am outspoken—most of the time to a fault. So you may trust that I mean what I say. Your actions have, in truth, been honorable and generous from the start."

"The tigress sheathing her claws? I would have thought you ready to tear me to shreds."

He sounded wounded, weary. It hurt her to hear his pain. "I do not mean to appear your enemy, sir. It has been some time since I wished to rip into your character." Her sigh stirred the raven locks curling at his collar. "I know I am all sharp edges and razored teeth. I—I can't seem to help it."

"You are rarely wrong in your assessments, Miss Kirtland. However, in judging your own assets, you have no notion of how far from the truth you are," His hands framed her face, then slowly slid upward to twine in the knot of her hair.

"Damnation," he whispered. "I am not sure this is a lesson we should explore."

There was no question that he was right. Yet practical, pragmatic Eliza found herself refusing to listen to reason. She tilted her head to meet his lidded gaze. "Why not?"

A hairpin fell to the carpet. Then another.

"Eliza," he murmured, as her tresses tumbled over her shoulders. "Lord, have you any idea how lovely you look with your hair loosened?"

Lovely?

"Y—you have left off your spectacles, sir—"

"My name is Marcus. I should like for you to say it."

Her lips quivered, but before they could form the first sound he stilled them with a kiss.

The taste of him was dizzying, potent. A lick of fire raced through her limbs. To keep her knees from buckling, Eliza clung more tightly to him, reveling in the hard, sloping strength of his shoulders and the reassuring breadth of his chest.

Lud, it felt wonderful to be so weak with desire. No wonder so many young girls fell from grace.

The window casement helped to keep her upright. Hips pressed against the ledge, she arched into his embrace, opening her mouth to the heady new sensations. As the earl deepened his kiss, he began caressing her breasts through the thin muslin—slow, swirling strokes that teased the tips to points of fire.

Eliza let out a soft cry. As heat surged through her, spiraling down to pool in her most intimate core, she let herself melt against him. Their bodies pressed close and she was acutely aware of his unmistakable maleness.

But rather than feel daunted or dismayed at arousing the earl's passions, Eliza felt deliciously wicked and wanton.

And wonderful.

No matter a part of her warned that it was wrong, she wanted more. More.

To the devil with being prim, practical Eliza Kirtland.

She held very still for an instant, then shook off any doubts. For once in her life, she meant to cast all caution to the wind and experience a taste of pure, primal passion.

As if sensing her tiny hesitation, Marcus pulled away. "Eliza..." Gently but firmly, he started to loosen her embrace.

"I know I have none of the practiced charms of a Diamond of the First Water," she stammered, "but—"

Her halting words were interrupted by a tentative knock at the door.

* * *

Hell and damnation. Marcus waited a fraction before answering. "On second thought, we will take tea in the drawing room," he called, stalling for an extra moment of reprieve.

Eliza had managed to retrieve most of her hairpins and was making a stab at taming the disorder of her dress.

"It is I, sir," said his nephew.

Tugging the folds of his cravat into some semblance of order, Marcus crossed the carpet and opened the door halfway. "Ah, so it's you, Lucien." He crossed his arms, using his frame to shield Eliza from view, and inclined a nod, but made no move to step aside.

"Might I have a word with you? I am sorry for interrupting, but it's rather important."

"Then do come in." He hoped he did not look as guilty as a spotty-faced schoolboy caught pilfering pastries. "Miss Kirtland and I were just going over some figures."

To his relief, Lucien looked too preoccupied with his own concerns to notice the air of tension in the room.

Out of the corner of his eye, Marcus saw that Eliza had managed to straighten her bodice and take a seat at the desk. Clearing her throat, she began fumbling through the estate papers.

"As I was saying, sir, the unexpected expenses for rebuilding the stable will be considerable," she said loudly, her voice a trifle more brittle than usual. "We may have to defer some other projects. And there won't be any profits from the estate until the first harvests."

The announcement gave his nephew pause for thought. "If you are looking to augment income, you might consider investing in the Exchange. There are some short term opportunities that offer a good return without undo risk."

The earl could not hide his surprise.

"I have always had more of an interest in cerebral challenges, "explained Lucien. "Rather than cutting a dash on horseback or mastering the fine points of fencing, I spend my time trying to hone my understanding of economics and politics. Mayhap you think me a man-milliner for it, but so it is."

"On the contrary, Lucien. I am...impressed. Perhaps you might offer a few suggestions."

"Thank you, sir. I shall be happy to look into the possibilities and see what I might recommend." His nephew resumed his limp toward the leather chair. "But that is not why I am here. Meredith and I were talking earlier and, well, I fell to thinking about our assumptions regarding our enemy..."

As he bent down to pick up something from the carpet, Eliza's face colored to the same shade of crimson in the Oriental design.

"...And how to apply logic."

Marcus was seized by the irrational urge to snatch the hairpin from his nephew's hand and stuff it in his pocket. Lucien, however, merely placed it on the desk as he passed by.

"I mean, it is logical to think that the man we seek is a gentleman with a past grudge against you, sir. But what if we look at it from another perspective? What if it is about Killingworth Manor, and not you personally?"

"Hmmm." Eliza's embarrassment appeared to fade somewhat in light of Lucien's suggestion.

Forgetting his other distractions, Marcus considered the idea. "Go on," he encouraged.

Lucien was quick to oblige. "The more I thought about what you said earlier, the more it made sense, sir—why would an enemy from Town choose here and now to exact revenge? It's *not* logical. The odds would be stacked against him, and our adversary, whatever his other faults, is not stupid."

At the earl's nod, he continued on. "So, with that in mind, who is the most obvious suspect?"

"Hastings." Both Marcus and Eliza spoke at the same time.

"Hastings," agreed Lucien. "No doubt it came as a nasty shock to learn you meant to take up a more permanent residence at Killingworth Manor. And when he discovered that you were actually taking an interest in the estate's management, he must have realized it was just a matter of time until his embezzlement of funds came to light."

"The same thoughts had occurred to me," said Marcus. "And yet, the truth is, I don't see how he could have been responsible for the attack on Miss Meredith or the other girl. Only a gentleman of the *ton* would know about Wolf's Head Society, and the details of its tattoo and what it stands for."

"But that is just it. Hastings *did* know."

"How?"

Lucien shot an apologetic look at Eliza before answering. "Several weeks ago, there was a night I did not return to the Manor until well after dawn. Needless to say, I had been drinking heavily —so heavily that I had cast up my accounts—and I stopped at the horse trough to clean myself up before slinking up to my room. Hastings saw me and offered commiseration, along with some soap and a towel.

He paused to think. "My memory is a bit hazy, but I do recall that he asked a number of questions and I was happy to oblige. He seemed especially curious about the mark on my breast and what it signified." His mouth tugged into a grimace. "At the time, his interest in me seemed nothing more than an effort to be friendly—which I welcomed. Now, of course, it appears in a much more sinister light."

"Bloody hell," murmured the earl softly

"You think I am right, Uncle Marcus?"

"I think you have hit it bang on the mark." Marcus started to pace. "But to prove it, we are going to have to catch him in the act."

"How?" It was Eliza who echoed his earlier question. With an errant curl caressing her cheek and a lushness clinging to her kiss-ravaged lips, she looked achingly lovely.

And achingly vulnerable.

Greed, made even more volatile by hatred—Hastings had been utterly ruthless in his earlier attacks. It was only by mere luck that none of them had yet been lethal. The next strike...

Marcus repressed an inward shiver. He couldn't allow there to be a next strike.

"As to that," he answered, "it may take me another day or two to work out the final plan." Marcus looked away, his voice taking on a rougher edge than he had intended. "But catch him we will."

"What can I do to help?" asked his nephew.

"You have already proved invaluable in identifying the villain. But for the moment, there is nothing that either of you can do." A sidelong glance at Eliza prompted him to add, "Save to keep a watchful eye open and not to stray far from the Manor alone."

"Very well, sir," replied Lucien. "Then I will let you get back to your figures, sir."

Was it his imagination, or did his nephew have the audacity to wink as he went by?

"An excellent suggestion." Eliza grabbed up a book on crop rotation and made to follow.

"I did not think we were quite finished here, Miss Kirtland," he said very softly.

"Oh, I believe we covered all the essentials, sir. The rest can wait for another time."

"Eliza..." The sound was no louder than the whispery brush of her skirts against his boots as he angled to cut off her line of retreat.

She avoided any eye contact. "I—I need to review several of these ledgers before my meeting with Whitney."

Perhaps she was right. Perhaps they both could use an interval of solitude to reschool their emotions.

Reluctantly, he stepped sideways and allowed her to pass.

* * *

ELIZA STARED DOWN AT THE DETAILED DIAGRAM OF properly furrowed soil. *Ha!* If only a hole would open up deep enough in the earth for her to drop all the way to Cathay. Yet not even the thought of vast oceans between them could dampen her burning mortification.

Or her simmering desire.

What a fool she must have appeared—an aging spinster clinging to the coat of a sinfully handsome rake. To his credit, Marcus—no, she must only think of him as Killingworth—had been kind. He had not sought to humiliate her, even though her fumbling inexperience must have been pitifully obvious to a man of his amatory prowess.

She pressed a tentative touch to her lower lip. He had kissed her, to be sure, but that did not signify overly much. She was wise enough in the ways of the world to know that men had primal urges—and the earl embodied the very essence of masculinity. For him, their intimate interlude had most likely been merely a passing fancy. While she might savor the lingering traces of his spice, he was no doubt grateful that his nephew's knock had extricated him from an awkward position.

Eliza had seen it in his eyes—the odd flicker in his eyes as he pulled away. It could only have been embarrassment.

Even odder was the fact that she felt no shame, just an ache of regret. As it wasn't likely that she would ever again experience a man's passionate kisses, she had wanted more.

Of what?

Of Marcus. Of his strength, his smile, his passion, his intelligence. No matter that she knew it was absurd to indulge in such a schoolgirl fantasy.

Giving up all pretense of reading a stick-in-the-mud passage on digging dirt, Eliza put the book aside and began to pace the perimeter of her bedchamber. Just as unsettling as the earl's kisses was the look in his eyes on hearing Lucien's revelation. She was sure he meant to set himself up as his former steward's next target. A prickling chill coursed down her spine, as if cold steel had touched bare flesh. Marcus was, by all accounts, a crack pugilist and a deadly shot. But he was also a gentleman, bound by a strict code of honor, and would fight fairly.

Hastings most definitely would not.

A thoroughly dirty dish, the man would have no compunction about chopping his own mother into mincemeat if he could see any profit from it.

Warning the earl would do little good. He was as damnably stubborn as she was about certain principles. Picking up her pace, Eliza started another circle of the room. It wasn't until she had passed the cheval glass for the third time that an angled reflection of her own scowl gave her pause for thought.

Unlike the earl, she was more of an even match for the former steward. She didn't fight fair either. Coming from the same world, Eliza understood his breed of men all too well. She was intimately acquainted with bullying creditors and intimidating tactics of petty tyrants who wished to keep her in her place. Like Hastings, she had no compunction about doing whatever it took to survive and keep her family from harm.

So, Eliza decided, it was up to her to see that Hastings was caught.

She owed it to the earl for her part in what had happened to Lucien. And for thinking the worst of him.

As for what she felt now...

Her heart gave a tiny lurch. It was best not to think of that, or the future. Triumph would be bittersweet—once the threat was over, her family would return to Rose Cottage and their old routine as if nothing had changed. Except that everything had changed. She had laughed at the idea of falling head over heels in love.

Love.

How ironic that the joke was on her.

She would, of course, take great pains to see that the earl never guessed the truth. Any further contact with him would be purely professional. The straitlaced steward had learned her lesson. She would take care never to let down her hair again.

It took another few turns of the room before Eliza distanced herself from disappointment and set to work devising a strategy. Her work with the area estates had made her familiar with much of the surrounding lands. If the former steward was indeed the culprit, she had a good idea of where he had gone to ground.

A surreptitious visit to his hiding place might turn up enough incriminating evidence to charge him with the previous crimes. Even if she were to encounter him, her walking through the woods would raise little suspicions. The Kirtland sisters were well-known for their foraging forays.

And if, on account of her association with Marcus, he sought to make her his next victim?

Her chin came up a fraction.

She would be ready to meet fire with fire. The earl had a very fine pistol in his desk drawer—the latest model from Manton's, according to his nephew. From the study it would be easy to slip unnoticed across the back terrace and out through the gardens.

* * *

"WHAT DO YOU MEAN SHE IS MISSING?" SETTING ASIDE A twinge of alarm, Marcus put down the set of drawings and stepped away from the men laboring over the new barn beams. "Miss Kirtland is with Whitney."

"I asked him, sir," replied Lucien. "Their meeting is scheduled for the morrow."

"Eliza is not in her bed chamber or the sick room, or the library," added Meredith.

"Or your study." His nephew's grim expression confirmed his growing fears. "I took the liberty of checking your desk drawer and your pistol is gone as well."

The earl swore. "Jem, saddle my horse," he called to the young groom. "And check if any of the other mounts are missing."

"I asked Whitney to make a search of the south fields, then report back here," said Lucien.

"Good thinking."

"Forgive me if I am acting skittish, sir." Meredith drew in a deep breath. "There may be a perfectly innocent explanation for her absence. She may have needed to fetch one of her own books or another shawl from home."

In which case, thought the earl, she would hardly need to lug along one of London's deadliest dueling weapons.

Damn the plaguey female and her fondness for firearms. He would take a birch to her backside if she had dared strike out on her own.

"I'll ride to Rose Cottage and see if she's there," volunteered Lucien.

"I'll go along, too," cried Meredith. "While you follow the lane, I can check along the shortcut—"

"No, damn it! All of you are to stay inside the Manor until I return." The earl flung himself into the saddle. "See that you keep her there, Lucien. Lock her in her room if need be."

"Yes, sir." His nephew's voice had the same taut grimness as his own.

"And show Whitney to the gun room when he arrives. Have him help you load and prime three of the hunting rifles. I want him and Robbie ready to ride out when I return."

Not waiting for an answer, he spurred his stallion into a gallop.

Fourteen

There was no sign of life in the gamekeeper's cottage. Nestled in a small clearing near the ocean cliffs, the small structure had not been used for years. Still, Eliza knew it to be in good repair, and despite its isolated position within the wooded grove, the place afforded quick access to the main footpaths running along the coast. A man could move about easily without attracting any notice.

After checking again for any telltale wisp of smoke, Eliza rearranged the folded cloth atop her basket and continued on down the sloping trail. The sleek butt and smooth trigger of the earl's weapon hidden within the wicker offered added reassurance that she was well prepared for any contingency. After all, she thought with a rueful quirk, she had not quailed at invading the earl's residence with naught but an ancient pistol whose aim was a touch erratic. She could manage a quick look around a single room without any trouble.

As she approached the door, footprints in the soft earth seemed to indicate she was on the right track. It was shut, and though a glance through the grimy panes of window glass showed no movement inside, she took the precaution of knocking.

Once, twice... On hearing no response, Eliza jiggled the latch. It was unlocked and cracked open at the nudge of her shoulder. She looked around, then ducked inside.

Someone was definitely in residence. Though the light was dim, and she dared not light a candle, she could make out the blankets lying on the bedstead, the cheese and bread in the open larder and the crockery on the makeshift table. Edging a step closer, she saw there was also a jumble of papers on the rough pine. A closer look showed the top one to be nothing more than an overdue accounting from a Portsmouth wine seller. But the next one proved a good deal more interesting.

Lamp oil—enough to light the tiny cottage for a year—a coil of rope, an ax. The bill proved nothing in itself, yet Eliza felt her pulse begin to quicken as she hurried through the rest of the pile. Hastings had made a careless mistake by leaving the papers lying about.

Perhaps he had made two by keeping an even more revealing document among them.

Hell's bells. As the last one fell from her fingers, she drew in a deep breath and slowly put the papers back in order. It was, she reminded herself, unreasonable to feel a stab of disappointment. The information on the lamp oil, while not outright proof, should be enough to convince the authorities to pursue an investigation of Hastings and his recent activities.

A cursory search of the lone cupboard turned up nothing else. Retracing her steps, Eliza reached out for the latch. But after a fraction of a pause, her hand suddenly veered for the coat hanging from the peg. No doubt the pockets would yield naught but lint, however it was worth a try.

Sure enough, she came away empty. Pulling a face, she was about to let the garment fall away when a faint crackle from near the collar drew her attention. Chiding herself for overlooking the breast pocket, she reached inside and withdrew a twist of string and a crumpled scrap of foolscap.

The sketch was crude, but unmistakable—the head of a wolf, jaws agape, teeth bared.

Eliza's first impulse was to tuck the incriminating evidence in her skirts and race back to the earl. But on recalling Lucien's mention of logic, she hesitated. Rushing off half-cocked was not always the wisest move—a lesson that ought to have been hammered home by now.

She forced herself to think rationally. If she took the paper with her, the authorities would have only her word of where it came from. On the other hand, if she left it…

Her fingers tightened, then she thrust it back into the coat and quickly stepped back out outside.

It took a moment for her eyes to adjust to the slanting sunlight. Still, she hurried blindly ahead, anxious to distance herself from the leering beast and all it stood for. In her haste, she stumbled on the stones.

But a grip on her arm kept her from falling.

"Why, fancy running into you here, Miss Kirtland."

* * *

MARCUS SLAMMED THE PARLOR DOOR SHUT. LIKE THE upstairs rooms of Rose Cottage, it was deserted, and Eliza's desk appeared undisturbed. He would make a quick check of the back garden, but he doubted it would turn up any trace of her.

Bloody hell. He should have anticipated trouble. His hand balled in a fist. Lud, if he lost her—

"What are you doing here? And where is Eliza?"

He whirled around to find Ned Laskin blocking the entrance-way. The farmer was carrying an ax and looked ready to use it. "That is what I am trying to determine," he replied through gritted teeth.

The other man made no move to let him pass. "The devil take

it, if you have harmed her in any way, I swear, I —I shall call you out!"

"Pitchforks at dawn?" Worry gave Marcus's voice an extra edge of sarcasm. Seeing Laskin go scarlet with anger, he raised a hand. "Look, I am not the devil you think, but I will be happy to meet you on the field of honor whenever you like—but not until Miss Kirtland is found. She has gone missing from the Manor, and if you wish to chop someone in half, I suggest you take that blade and help me search for Joseph Hastings."

"Hastings?" The farmer looked wary. "Why would he have any grudge against Eliza?"

Marcus ignored the question. "Any idea where he may be holed up?"

"Why Eliza?" demanded Ned.

The cursed fellow was proving as stubborn as one of his oxen. "Because she has taken it into her head to go after the man who is behind the spate of violence in the area."

"Hastings?" Laskin looked undecided on whether to believe him. But after a long moment, he growled, "One of the men in the village might know."

"Bloody hell, man! Then what in the name of Lucifer are you waiting for? Even a slowtop must be able to work out that she is in grave danger!"

His explosion of temper finally seemed to spark a grudging acceptance of the story. "Damnation," said Ned. "He has a vicious temper when crossed, and Eliza is not wont to back down—"

"Then we had best move quickly. Gather what men you can in the village and scour through the area east of the Manor. I will take charge of the west."

Once he was back in the saddle, the earl followed a shortcut through the fields, the thud of his heart matching the pounding pace of his lathered mount. He didn't need the farmer's warning to remind him of just how dangerous a man his former steward was. To Hastings, Eliza was merely a pawn in a game. He would sacrifice her to achieve his own goals with the same casual flick he would use to remove a piece of carved ivory from the black and white tiles of a chessboard.

The reins grew slippery with sweat. The earl was all too familiar with men obsessed with winning. A certain madness took hold of them. With each successive loss it grew worse. As he urged his stallion over a stone fence, Marcus searched his mind for how he might signal surrender. He realized he would give anything to get her back.

Whitney and his foreman were waiting with Lucien and Meredith in the stable yard. Seeing his face as he reined to a halt, they didn't bother to ask whether he had had any luck.

Brushing his wind-tangled locks from his brow, the earl looked to Meredith. "You're familiar with the woods and cliffs to the west. Where might Hastings be hiding?"

Meredith quickly named off several likely spots. "But I'll have to come along and show you. Their exact location is not easy to describe."

He gave a grim nod. "We can't chance a mistake."

"I am coming, too." Lucien handed him a rifle, and before the earl could argue, added, "If I cannot keep up, go ahead and leave me in the dust. But I'll not stay here while Eliza is in peril."

"Get your horses." Marcus had only one fight in mind. "And let us be off."

* * *

"How kind of you to pay a visit to my humble abode." The earl's former steward gave a mocking wave at the dilapidated structure. "Not quite the Manor House, as you have no doubt remarked, but then, not all of us are in His Lordship's good graces these days."

"I—I was just checking that no thief had broken into the cottage. Forgive me for trespassing. I will be on my way."

"What's the rush?" His lips curled, revealing a flash of teeth. "Now that you are here, won't you join me for a cup of tea."

"Thank you, but I am really rather late as it is." Eliza made a show of shifting her basket, hoping to free her arm. "I promised Dr. Laskins a fresh batch of ground willow bark for one of his patients."

Hastings did not loosen his hold. "Let him wait."

Fear squeezed at her chest. She couldn't quite reach the pistol. "Very well," she replied, forcing herself to stay calm. "I suppose it will do no harm to stay a little longer."

His bark of laughter was mirthless. "No—no harm at all."

He led her back inside. In the gloomy light, the place looked even more primitive than before. Eliza ventured a sidelong glance and saw that her captor's face was just as stripped of any civilizing veneer. She bit her lip. Her chances of escape were fast slipping away. She would have to make a move, and soon.

If only the earl were here to steady her trembling knees. If only it were his hands upon her, rather than the cold, reptilian touch of her captor. But if ever she wished to feel the warmth of his arms again—even if it was only to have him shake her from here to Hades for being such a fool—she was going to have to keep her wits alert.

The sooty shadows did not quite dim the malevolent glint in his eye as he indicated the only chair. "Have a seat. A pity I can't offer you all the fine comforts of Killingworth's house. It is easy to grow used to the trappings of luxury, is it not, Miss Kirtland? The fine china, the rich damasks, the aged brandy—" A nasty leer stretched across his mouth—"The carved four-poster bed."

"I am merely a guest under His Lordship's roof for a short time, Mr. Hastings." Eliza sought to allay his bitter suspicions. "And will soon return to my modest cottage."

"On the contrary." The former steward gave her another little push. "I think you have other plans."

His grip slipped slightly, and she seized the moment to twist away, at the same time reaching for the hidden pistol. The trigger was cool and solid against her finger. Steadying her nerve, she raised the barrel and swung it around.

She had moved quickly, but so had Hastings. His arm shot out, knocking the barrel's aim up to the ceiling. A shot rang out and a bullet splintered one of the beams.

"She-bitch." He punched her, the snap of the blow sending her reeling into the table.

Stunned, Eliza fell back on the rough planking. Before she could gather her wits, he was upon her, wrenching her hands behind her back. He was much stronger than she had imagined, his crude power so very different from the Marcus's firm measure of control.

She blinked back tears. Indeed, there was no comparison between the two men. At the Black Cat's first touch, she had known he had not an ounce of evil in him, while this beast...

Reminding herself of what he had done to Meredith and Lucien, she determined not to give in to despair. Not when there was still a breath left in her body to fight for seeing the miscreant brought to justice.

Hastings gave a last, painful tug to the rope he had knotted around her wrists, and shoved her down in the chair. "You and your righteous meddling in things no female ought to poke her nose in. Always stirring up trouble with your newfangled ideas and damnable ledgers."

"I never intended any ill—"

A slap silenced her. "You think me a fool? You come to Killingworth Manor and suddenly I am turned out of a lucrative position!" Grabbing a handful of her hair, he yanked back her head. "You should have minded your own business, Miss Kirtland. Now you are going to pay for interfering with me."

"It doesn't matter what you do to me. The earl knows you are the one responsible for all these crimes."

"He may suspect it, but he can't prove it." Hastings flashed a wolfish smile. "I've been too clever to leave any evidence."

"You have been clever," she conceded. The words nearly stuck in her throat, but perhaps she might turn his own vanity against him. So far, she admitted, it seemed his only weakness. "Exceedingly so. I take it your original plan was to take advantage of the earl's rakish reputation to stir up suspicions that he—or someone in his household—was preying on local girls. You hoped the hue and cry might drive him back to London, leaving you to enjoy the bounty of his estate, as you had been doing for some time."

"Aren't you the clever one yourself, Miss Kirtland," he sneered. "Yes, that is precisely what I had in mind. Mr. Harkness proved an easy mark. A weak, blabbering fool. The fact that he and the earl despise each other made it child's play to manipulate him."

Eliza did not disabuse him of that notion.

"Then *you* came along and had your own idea on how to profit from Killingworth's penchant for bedding women."

She drew in a sharp breath.

"My arse gets tossed in the mud, while yours lands in a fine tester bed. It hardly seems fair, does it?"

"You are mistaken." Her voice was a taut whisper. "I assure you, the earl has no interest in me."

"Oh, I don't doubt that a shrewish country spinster has few charms to attract a notorious rake," agreed Hastings. "But as I made it my business to know his habits, I am aware that it has been a long time since His Lordship had a woman in his bed. I imagine he would take his pleasure with anything that wore a skirt."

Argument seemed pointless.

"As I said, it doesn't seem fair."

"I have learned over the years that life is rarely fair, Mr. Hastings. One must learn to deal with disappointment."

"Why should I?" His face twisted in anger.

"Surely you've a handsome sum tucked away from your

embezzlement. Why not take it and flee to some distant place where you can live to enjoy it," she asked.

"Be a sheep and meekly accept my fate? Not when I am smart enough to do something about it. I want more and I intend to get it."

"Perhaps you are not so smart as you think."

A nasty laugh echoed the slap of his palm on her cheek. "I'd watch my mouth if I were you. You are hardly in a position to comment on my intelligence, seeing as you blundered straight into my arms."

That was the one thing on which she and the devil saw eye to eye. "What do you intend to do with me? It won't be long before I am missed at the Manor."

Hastings took some time to consider the question. Stepping away from the chair, he circled the table, lips pursed in thought. After several turns, a slow grin indicated he had reached a decision. "The footpaths are notoriously unstable this times of year. A pity you chose to wander too close to the edge while looking for your blasted berries."

"Another accident?" Eliza tried to keep the tremor of fear from her voice. If push came to shove, she knew she didn't have the strength to resist. "The earl will know it was foul play."

"But again, he won't be able to prove it." The former steward yanked her to her feet. "You have been a cursed nuisance, Miss Kirtland. With you out of the way, I can bide my time and pick the right moment for my next move against Killingworth. And this time, I'll make sure that my plans aren't spoiled by a nosy chit."

"You think he will stand by and wait for you to strike again? He will hunt you down."

"Let him try. So far, the Black Cat has been a toothless tabby."

<h1 style="text-align:center">Fifteen</h1>

The tinge of red in the scudding clouds added a new shade of urgency to their search. The sun was setting fast, and if night came before they found Eliza, the earl didn't dare think of what might happen during the stretch of blackness between dusk and dawn.

He left off his survey of the horizon. "That is the last spot on these hills. What is left?"

"Two places," replied Meredith quickly. She, too, was eyeing the deepening colors of the sky. "But they are in opposite directions. There is no way we can get to both before darkness falls."

"Then we must split up," said Lucien decisively. Though his face was deathly pale beneath the dust and sweat, he had hung in gamely over the bruising ride. "Uncle Marcus?"

The earl nodded. Loath though he was to accept it, his nephew was right. "Which do you think he has chosen?"

She hesitated, but only for an instant. "The cliffs."

"Whitney, you and Robbie will check the caves, while we head on to the cliffs."

The two men listened intently to Meredith's description.

"I need not warn you to go carefully. If you have a clear shot, take it. But otherwise..." he didn't bother to finish. They all knew the alternative was prayer.

The freshening wind and the sound of the rising surf muffled their approach to the clearing. Still, Marcus signaled for them to dismount and continue on foot. Handing his rifle to Lucien, more as a crutch than anything else, he quickly checked the priming of his pistols. At close range, they would be far more effective weapons.

"Watch your step," he warned, tucking one away in his coat pocket. At the first stumble, he meant to leave his nephew behind, even if it meant lashing him to the nearest oak.

The way was clear enough and they quickly crested the wooded slope. Half hidden in the lengthening shadows, the hut looked as if it hadn't been disturbed in ages.

Marcus eased back the hammer. "Wait here. I'll have a look."

The scuffed earth, the unlatched door—someone else had been here, and recently. Holding his breath, he nudged the door open a crack wider.

"Damnation."

The earl wasn't aware that he had spoken aloud until Lucien and Meredith, breathless from their headlong run, appeared at his shoulder.

"Too late," he added, stepping inside and surveying the tumbled basket and overturned chair.

"That is Eliza's basket," whispered Meredith.

He already knew that, for the staleness of the air could not quite overpower the lingering trace of verbena and lavender. "Damnation," he repeated. "Damn, damn, damn."

Lucien could not repress his own oath on catching sight of the pistol barrel under the bedstead. "It's been fired," he said, brushing the grains of powder from his fingertips. His eyes swept over the floor. "But," he was quick to add, "I see no sign of blood."

Thank God for small miracles, thought Marcus. An involuntary glance heavenward revealed the splintered wood and jagged hole. The scenario flashed before his eyes—she had managed to draw the pistol, only to be overpowered by the superior strength and size of a male opponent.

Oh, if only she had learned her lesson the first time around.

"They have not been gone long." Meredith held up a sprig of wild thyme from the tangle of herbs. "Look, the leaves have not yet wilted."

The earl prayed that the same could be said of Eliza. "We may have a chance to catch up with them if we hurry. There is only one way they could have gone."

The sea.

His insides were churning like a storm-tossed ocean, crosscurrents of emotions colliding in a tempest of hope and fear. He had always been calm in the face of danger before. The choices had been his and his alone. That he could live with. But this gut-wrenching worry was something he had never experienced before.

Perhaps because he had never been in love. His past affairs had been fleeting—flesh touching flesh, nothing deeper.

But Eliza Kirtland had gotten under his skin. Her fierce loyalty, her sharp intelligence, her gritty courage had slowly but surely won his heart. He couldn't quite imagine life without her there by his side, demanding he measure up to his own expectations.

Indeed, they made an odd couple, for he believed that he, too, had helped her to see another side of herself. There was passion beneath the rigid columns of numbers. That was part of life's equation, and judging from their first lesson, she was a quick study.

Work and play. Killingworth Manor could be a real home, filled with countless possibilities for happiness, for a family, for a future. All the things he had never valued before.

Lord, let him find her. He had never even told her of his feelings.

The evening mists had not yet floated up from the water, yet he moved as if in fog, finding it hard to breathe, hard to think.

But think he must. Time enough later for regrets, recriminations.

"Uncle Marcus." Lucien's low call slowed his steps.

As he looked around, Marcus noticed that his hands were bleeding from scrabbling up the steep path that cut between the outcroppings of granite. He nodded and continued on at a more measured pace. Another twisting turn and they would be within a stone's throw of the cliff top.

* * *

IF ONLY.

The words seemed to crash against the inside of Eliza's head with the same incessant rhythm of the waves pounding the rocks below. She rarely indulged in pining over the past. The worries of the present and the future were usually daunting enough to keep her mind fully occupied.

Being useful, she reminded herself.

That thought seemed to mock her every move of late. At least she had, for a fleeting interlude, shoved her ledgers and her everyday troubles aside and allowed herself a taste of passion. She would take the earl's kiss to the grave and beyond, savoring the warmth of its intimacies, the sweetness of sharing a connection of body and spirit.

Nothing could take that from her. Not the bruising grip on her arm or the muttered threats that harangued her to move faster over the steep stones.

"Clumsy cow." Hastings jerked her upright and with another crude oath shoved her forward.

Eliza controlled the urge to fight back. She was not after a moral victory, but a far more pragmatic one. There was no doubt he could knock her senseless. The only reason he had not done so was to save himself the trouble of hauling the deadweight of her unconscious body along the narrow path. So she would march along meekly and watch for the one slip that might give a chance to break free.

"Not much farther," he taunted. "Let me think, I believe I shall leave your shawl artfully arranged on a snag of rock, in case your body is never fished out from the pounding surf."

She smiled, hoping a show of calm would goad him into a temper. Anger often clouded judgment.

"An excellent idea. I trust the hangman will be equally artful in arranging a knot of hemp around your neck once the earl has seen you charged with the crimes of assault, arson, and murder. I may be feeding the crabs, but you will be carrion for the crows. They tend to leave a murderer's carcass dangling from the gibbet until it's pecked clean."

The sting of the slap was worth seeing his face contort in rage. "You think the earl is going to care about the disappearance of his doxie? I don't see him rushing to your rescue. I wager he already has another wench warming his sheets. But not for long. He'll pay for his pride."

She stopped his gloating with a quick retort. "If you have been truly clever, you would have used your head instead of your fists when it came to Killingworth's nephew. You call him a stupid boy, but he is the earl's heir, you know. I, for one, would have realized the opportunity for a profitable partnership and made friends with him, rather than be so short-sighted as to frame him for a crime."

It was almost amusing to see the man's face fall as the import of her words sunk in. His lips moved—counting, no doubt, all the guineas he let slip through his fingers by not having thought of the idea himself.

"So that was your game?" Hastings finally snarled. "Bedding the nephew and not the earl?"

Eliza didn't deign to answer the despicable question

"Well, either way, you chose a losing proposition when you thought you could usurp my place at the Manor," he said. "Did you really think I was going to give up such bounty so easily?"

"I didn't realize it was yours to give," she replied.

Cursing, he pushed her again. With her hands bound, Eliza fell awkwardly against the rocks, banging her knees and shoulder. But she managed to cup a shard of granite between her palms before he wrenched her upright. As a weapon it was hardly a match for his knife. And yet, she reminded herself, David had slain Goliath with naught but a pebble.

The path was winding closer and closer to the precipice. She knew she would have to strike soon.

* * *

THE TWO SHAPES STOOD OUT IN SHARP SILHOUETTE, dark as slate against the purpling sky. Marcus watched for a moment, heart beating like a hammer against his ribs, as their pace along the path slowed because of the treacherous footing.

He climbed a little higher, angling off the path for a clearer view of Eliza and her captor. "Let her go, Hastings." Waves crashed against the rocks, nearly drowning out his shout.

His former steward whipped around, the wind carrying his first words out to sea. The next, however, sailed loud and clear. "Never!"

"You have won. Name whatever price you like—money, a boat to France. It's all yours if you release Miss Kirtland."

"You think I am a bloody fool?"

"You have my word of honor that you will go free."

Hastings replied with a jeering curse. "You want your bit of muslin? Come get her."

Marcus measured the distance. No way could he reach them before his former steward made it to the edge of the cliff. "You are right—you are no fool. So think on it, Miss Kirtland is your only bargaining chip." He flashed his pair of pistols. "If she comes to any harm, you're a dead man in the next instant."

He saw Hastings hesitate and consider the situation.

"Perhaps you are right." The former steward yanked Eliza around to serve as a shield and held a knife perilously close to her neck. "I assume you have come on horseback."

"Yes," answered the earl, his finger hovering in frustration above the trigger of his weapon. He was a crack shot, and Hastings's head was exposed just enough...

But no. He had bought some time and would wait for a better chance. He would rather tear the man limb from limb with his bare hands.

"Throw down your weapons," ordered Hastings, pointing to a deep crevasse in the splintered rocks. "In there. Then we will come down. Once I'm well away from the village I'll let her go." A pause. "You have my word of honor."

Which was, thought Marcus, worth less than spit.

Nonetheless, he did as he was told. "You'll get no trouble from me." He looked around to order his nephew to do the same, but Lucien was nowhere in sight.

Meredith had started to climb up to join him, and the look in her eyes caused the question he was about to ask to die on his lips.

"I'm unarmed as well," she called to Hastings. "Our two horses are yours for the taking."

Fisting a hand in Eliza's cloak, the former steward pushed her forward. "Step back off the path," he ordered, and put your hands atop your head so I can see that you're not up to no good."

As Marcus watched their slow progress down through the loose stones, he tried to force his thoughts away from the sharpened steel at her throat and concentrate on how he was going to free her from the madman's clutches. He would only have a split second to act.

And no second chance.

* * *

"HASTINGS."

At first Eliza thought it was merely the whisper of the wind playing tricks with her ears. But when it came again, her captor yanked her to a halt. Out of the corner of her eye, she saw Lucien crouched behind an outcropping of granite.

"Back off." Hastings pushed the blade right up against her throat. "Put down that bloody rifle or I swear, I'll hurt her."

"As if I give a fig what you do to her," said Lucien in a nasty drawl. "She and my bloody uncle are making my life hell—so I've got a proposition for you."

Hastings darted a look at the earl, who was standing still as a statue, and then wet his lips. "I'm listening."

"You're a diabolical bastard—but a very clever diabolical bastard. I need someone with brains and daring. So I'm willing to forget about all the trouble you caused me because between you and my uncle, you're the lesser of two evils."

"Go on."

"I say we make a deal and become partners. We get rid of my uncle with a quick bullet and lo, I'm the earl's heir and with him out of the way, Killingworth Manor is mine. I'll rehire you to run it—we'll have a binding bond, for neither of us can betray the other without putting a noose around his own neck."

"You are cleverer than I thought, Mr. Harkness."

Yes, he is, thought Eliza.

"I could learn much from you."

Hasting tightened his grip on her arm. "What about Miss Kirtland and her sister?"

"Toss them over the cliff, along with my uncle's carcass, once we put a bullet in his brain." Still hidden by the rocks, Lucien held out the rifle by its barrel. "Here, you had better take it," he muttered, nearly dropping the heavy weapon. "I'm still too weak to aim the damn thing. And I'm a poor shot."

The rifle butt was out of his reach. Hastings gauged the distance, then Eliza felt the blade leave her throat as he darted sideways to grab it.

It all seemed to happen in a blur—in the same instant Lucien sprang up and swung the weapon in a tight arc.

The heavy wood stock smacked against the former steward's skull with a resounding *crack*.

Hastings dropped to the ground like a sack of stones.

"*That*," said Lucien forcefully, "was for Miss Meredith."

As Hastings twitched and tried to raise his head, a swift kick caught him flush on the jaw, knocking him unconscious.

"And *that* was for Miss Kirtland." Lucien dropped the weapon and reached out to untie Eliza's wrists, but stumbled and dropped to his knees, the last of his strength ebbing away. "Sorry," he said with a wry gasp "A fine hero I make, falling into a half faint, but—"

"Oh, Mr. Harkness..." Eliza sunk down beside him and steadied his shoulder with her bound hands. "You are quite the most wonderful hero in the world."

"I am?" He sounded a little dazed.

"Indeed, you are." Marcus skidded to a halt and crouched down to enfold both of them in a hard hug. "Thank God," he whispered, giving one last squeeze before releasing them and reaching for the fallen knife to cut away the rope around Eliza's wrists.

"No doubt you have a few far less flattering names to fling at me, sir," she murmured as he carefully saw at the knots. "Which I sorely deserve. I'm so sorry—"

"Let us save recriminations for later," he interrupted. "Right now, all that matters is to get both of you back to the Manor, where you can be tended to properly."

"I'm not injured in the least—save for my pride," responded Eliza haltingly. She was still feeling a little dizzy from the spin of last few moments. "I—I thought I was being so clever, and yet what I did was put all of you at terrible risk."

"As I said, we'll discuss that later." Marcus put his arms around her and gently drew her to her feet. "Come, let me take you down to where the horses are waiting." Shooting a glance at Hastings, who lay unmoving among the sharp stones, he began unknotting his cravat. "Just as soon as I bind this cur hand and foot so that Whitney and Robbie may haul his miserable carcass to the magistrate."

"You should be assisting Mr. Harkness," protested Eliza.

"Mr. Harkness," he murmured, "has no need of me for assistance." His mouth quirked into a faint smile as he watched Meredith minister to his nephew. "I think he is in good hands."

With much cooing and clucking, her sister helped Lucien to his feet. Sliding her arm around his waist, she looked around to Eliza. "Thank God you are safe! I shall envelop you in hugs, just as soon as I get Luc—Mr. Harkness down from here. I fear his overexertions may bring on a relapse of fever."

"I'm fine," grumbled Lucien as he swayed against Meredith's shoulder. "Just need a moment to catch my breath."

"You two go right ahead," replied Marcus. "I shall see that your sister makes it down from these cliffs without further mishap."

"I'm sorry," repeated Eliza as he finished trussing up Hastings. She wished she could see his eyes—his voice was coolly calm, giving no hint of what emotions he might be feeling.

Other than relief that her disobeying his orders hadn't resulted in utter disaster.

A shiver coursed down her spine as she thought again of how her impetuous actions had put all of them at risk.

"I'm sorry, too." Marcus rose and dusted his hands. They were, she saw, badly scraped. "Sorry that I didn't figure things out sooner. Sorry that I didn't act faster to protect you from such a terrible ordeal."

He stepped closer, close enough that she could see the tiny lines of worry etched on his windblown face. "Sorry that I—"

A touch of her fingertips to his lips silenced him. "As you said, sir, time enough for recriminations later—and God knows, I shall have plenty of them. But for the moment, let us simply give thanks that we are all safe and unharmed."

"Agreed." He stared off into the distance for a brief moment, as if searching the churning seas beyond the cliffs for something further to add. But then, with a wordless exhale, he merely offered his arm, and they started slowly down the path.

For an interlude, there was naught but the sounds of the wind gusting through the rocks and the scuffling crunch of stones beneath their feet. Eliza kept her gaze locked straight ahead, though she would have liked to steal a peek at the earl's profile.

But then again, she decided, his expression would likely be no more revealing of inner emotion than the surrounding slabs of granite. He hid his feelings well—which might be for the best, given her recent impetuous actions. No doubt he was bitterly regretting the twist of fate that had brought her intrusion into his life.

She felt her shoulders slump. His world had been turned on its ear—

"You must be exhausted, Miss Kirtland." Marcus slipped a steadying arm around her waist. "Allow me to be of more support."

"I don't wish to impose on you further, sir," Eliza mumbled. "I've been enough of an onerous burden." *Crunch, crunch.* As if echoing her unsettled mood, the shards of stone shifted beneath her half boots. "Not to speak of all the ill I've brought down on you and your household."

"I should say the good you have wrought far outweighs the ill. The circumstances have brought out the best in Lucien..."

And they have brought out the best in you, she couldn't help thinking to herself.

"Your sister's kindness and compassion have been powerful reasons for that as well," added Marcus in a thoughtful voice. "I wonder..."

Eliza finally ventured a glance at his face and saw he was watching the couple ahead of them pick their way down the steep path.

"I wonder if the sham announcement we circulated might come to have any truth to it?"

"I think it possible," replied Eliza. "I believe the two of them have come to have a genuine regard for each other."

He turned his head and finally their eyes met. "And is that unwelcome to you?"

"No, not at all," said Eliza softly. "I have learned a number of invaluable lessons over these last few weeks, foremost among them the perils of rushing to judgment."

The earl took a moment to guide their steps around a rough patch of rocks before answering, "I, too, have learned some invaluable lessons."

She found herself holding her breath, waiting for him to go on.

His mouth gave a wry twitch. "I can now add and subtract columns of numbers correctly, and know the going market price for mangelwurzels and alfalfa. Among other useful skills."

Useful. The air leaked out of her lungs in a soundless sigh. What had she expected? A more intimate admission, just because he had once bestowed a casual kiss?

"You are an excellent teacher," added Marcus after a hint of hesitation.

"Well, it is heartening to know that I can, on occasion, be useful." She tried to match his tone, but her voice came out a little sharper than she intended.

His brows rose slightly, but Eliza hardly noticed. Fatigue seemed to have overpowered her senses, for all of a sudden she was too tired to think, too tired to speak, too tired to feel anything but a dull ache in her chest.

He seemed to feel the change come over her, for he drew her closer, his hold tightening. "We're almost there," he murmured. "Can you hold up for just a short while longer?"

"But of course," replied Eliza, keeping her eyes on the dust swirling around her skirts. "One of the lessons I learned long before I intruded upon your life was never to count on having a shoulder to lean on. So no need to worry about me—I'll survive."

Sixteen

"Well, it seems the troubles are finally over," said Meredith as she set a hand on Lucien's arm to steady his steps down the terrace stairs and onto the graveled walkway.

Whitney had joined them in the breakfast room that morning, and over a bountiful meal of shirred eggs and gammon, he had made a full report on the aftermath of the cliffside confrontation.

"Yes, we need not fear that Hastings will ever hurt anyone again," replied Lucien. "The magistrate has him safely locked up until the next assizes, and what with the evidence of his heinous crimes, it seems likely he will be sent to the gallows." He set his jaw. "I am not a bloodthirsty person, but I shall be sorely tempted to dance a jig on his grave."

"The monstrous acts he did were purely for greed and self-interest, so it is difficult to feel any compassion," she answered. "But everyone, even a man with such a twisted soul, deserves a bit of pity."

He heaved a heavy sigh. "You are far too kind. As I well know."

"Good heavens, it is *you* who have displayed a kindness of

heart, not to speak of extraordinary courage," responded Meredith, noting that her praise brought a tinge of color to his face. "Why, you risked your life for Eliza, even though you had a right to blame her for your own travails."

"Your sister was only trying to protect her loved ones," he said. "And yet, even when she thought me a vile monster, both she and you did not hesitate to help me when no one else would."

"Perhaps," she murmured, "at heart, we both sensed that you were not evil."

"The devilish thing was, I wasn't even sure myself," he said haltingly.

"Mr. Harkness—"

"Lucien," he corrected. "I—I would hope that by now, we are good enough friends to dispense with formalities."

"I..." Meredith felt herself color under his gaze. "I have long thought of you as a friend, L-Lucien."

"I am very glad to hear it." He paused as they started through the archway leading into the rose gardens and leaned back against the stones. The shadows dipped and darted over his face, obscuring all but the faint gleam of light in his eyes. "Actually, I hope we are more than friends, Meredith." He cleared his throat. "Though I hardly dare to think it might be possible."

"That is because you are far too modest." A smile tremored on her lips. "I think you are quite the most wonderful man I have ever met."

He blinked, hope and joy shining through his lashes. "Y-you do?"

Meredith touched a hand to his cheek. "I do."

"By Jove," he said faintly. "That gives me courage to ask the next question. Would you—could you—ever consider...making our sham betrothal, um, more than a sham?"

Though his stuttering was rather sweet, she decided to help put an end to his verbal struggling. "Are you, perchance, asking me to marry you, Lucien?"

A boyish grin slowly blossomed on his face. "Well, yes, that's exactly what I'm doing, but I'm making a mull of it." He edged forward a step, just enough to lean around and pluck a red rose from one of the nearby bushes.

"Here, let me start over, and do it properly." He dropped down to one knee. "I love you, Meredith, more than words can express. Will you be my wife?"

She knelt down beside him and wrapped her arms around his shoulders. "Yes. But only if you will rise before you reinjure your ribs and bring on another attack of fever."

"I would expire a deliriously happy man," Lucien murmured. He leaned in and ever so gently pressed his lips to hers for a long, lingering moment. "But yes, perhaps it's better to stand. I would rather survive to enjoy years and years of wedded bliss."

Together they rose.

"For we will be happy, my love," he whispered.

"I have no doubt of that," she answered, holding him close and tilting her mouth up for another kiss. For a time they stood entwined, the delicate floral scent accentuating the ethereal sweetness of their happiness.

They might, thought Meredith, have remained there for hours had not Lucien's hound chosen that moment to bound up and drop a stick at his master's feet with a playful bark.

"I am always happy to oblige you, Ajax." Lucien flung the stick out to the far lawns. "After all, it was you who helped bring us together."

"Clever hound," said Meredith.

"Yes, it only took me several hours and several pocketfuls of beef morsels to train him to jump up on a swirl of feminine skirts."

"Clever fellow."

"I thought so." Lucien grinned, but it quickly gave way to a cough. "Er, I guess we had better go inside and announce the news. I confess, I am a trifle nervous about your sister's reaction. If she doesn't approve—"

"If she doesn't approve, she will learn to approve," said Meredith softly but decisively.

His mouth quirked up at the corners. "You have her same steel, you just keep it better hidden."

Meredith ran a fingertip over one of the rose petals. "Eliza has always felt that she had to be tough and strong to protect Mama and me."

"I hope she will let me share in those duties now," he replied quietly. "Not that she needs any help—why, even Uncle Marcus is a trifle intimidated by her."

The comment brought a laugh to her lips. "When it comes to the ledgers and farm management, she does have a knack of taming the Black Cat's growls." She paused for a moment. "But you know, I don't think either is intimidated by each other's show of claws. In fact, I think they rather enjoy their arguments."

"The same thought had occurred to me," mused Lucien. He paused to throw the stick for Ajax again before adding, "Do you think that might be a sign of a deeper mutual attraction?"

Meredith took her time in considering the question. "Yes, I do, but I don't think either is willing to admit it—not even to themselves. Both my sister and His Lordship keep their innermost feelings well-guarded. So whether they will dare to trust their hearts to another is not something I can say for sure."

She pressed the rose to her cheek and felt the silky softness of its petals caress against her skin. "For their sakes, I hope they decide the risk is worth it."

"So do I," said Lucien. "I think they would make a perfect couple." He flashed another grin. "A lady who dares to pull a pistol on the Black Cat is just the sort of companion Uncle Marcus needs."

"I couldn't agree more," replied Meredith softly. "But they must come to that conclusion themselves."

"True." He offered his arm. "Well, let us go set an example for them. Perhaps they will take the hint."

* * *

ELIZA SET HER CANDLE DOWN ON THE DESK AND OPENED the ledger. Supper had been a festive meal, with the happy couple toasted more than a few times with champagne brought up from the earl's cellar. She smiled, recalling the look of bliss on her sister's face. And Lucien—the way he had looked on Meredith throughout the meal left no doubt in her mind that the marriage was a perfect match of hearts.

Whoever would have imagined such a thing several months ago?

"Not me," Eliza murmured, as she, sharpened her quill and uncapped the inkwell.

Which only proved how unreliable her own judgment was.

The thought turned the lingering sparkle of the wine a trifle flat, but she shook off the sensation and began to study the accounts. Work was always a welcome distraction from personal feelings.

At least she could make the columns of numbers add up.

"The monthly expenses can wait until morning, Miss Kirtland."

Eliza jerked her head up in surprise at the sound of the earl's voice. She hadn't heard his steps in the corridor.

"This is supposed to be an evening of celebration."

"Meredith and Lucien are taking a starlit stroll in the gardens, so they are quite happy to celebrate on their own," she replied.

"They do seem over the moon." Rather than retreat, Marcus came into the room and took a seat in the armchair by the hearth. Steepling his fingers on his chest, he gazed at the banked coals but said nothing more.

Eliza worked on for a few moments in silence before venturing a reply. "Your toasts were most gracious, for which I am very grateful. They truly love each other, but not many aristocrats would be thrilled by the idea of their heir marrying a nobody."

"Your sister is not a nobody," he said softly. "She possesses a nobility far greater than any paper title can confer."

"As I said, my family is very fortunate that you are willing to look beyond convention." Even to her own ears, the reply sounded awfully prim, but on watching the pale flickers of light play over his profile, she found her throat was too tight to manage any other sound. Biting her lip, she looked back down at the ledger.

"You sound surprised at that," he remarked. "You still think me an arrogant, self-absorbed rascal?"

For several long moments, the only answer was the scratch of her pen.

"Miss Kirtland?" he finally prompted.

Eliza turned the page. "I didn't think that required a reply. You know very well that it has been quite a while since I thought that."

"Do I?"

The conversation was taking a decidedly uncomfortable turn. "You hired me, sir," she pointed out. "No arrogant, self-absorbed rascal would have done that."

Marcus rose and poured himself a glass of brandy. "Why is it I feel I have just been damned with faint praise."

"You hardly need praise from me," replied Eliza.

He drained his glass in one gulp and refilled. There was an overbright glitter in his eyes that made her wonder whether he was in his cups.

"Perhaps you have had enough to drink, Killingworth," she added.

"Perhaps." To Eliza's dismay, he slowly crossed the carpet and perched a hip on the corner of the desk.

Her skin began to prickle.

"Or perhaps not." Marcus punctuated his words with a long swallow of the amber spirits.

Snapping the ledger's cover shut, she pushed back her chair. "You're right—this isn't a good evening for work. So if you will excuse me, I'll leave you to your revelries."

He put a hand on her shoulder. "Stay for a moment. I was hoping we might...talk."

Dangerous, dangerous, dangerous. Every instinct was telling her to flee, but she didn't wish to appear a coward. "Very well. What is it you wish to converse about?"

"All business, I see," he murmured under his breath.

"We *do* have a business arrangement, sir," Eliza pointed out.

"I am damnably aware of that." His tone turned tight. "Just as I am aware that you are back to using the formality of 'sir' and 'milord' when we—as you put it—converse."

"I am simply trying to maintain proprieties."

He let out a brusque laugh. "From the moment we first met and you aimed a pistol at my heart, there has been nothing remotely proper about our relationship."

"It was aimed a touch lower," said Eliza, trying to defuse the strange tension crackling through the air around them.

"Ha! You see," he responded. "No proper employee would dare to make sport of my nether regions."

"I..." Her gaze darted down to his breeches, which fit his contoured thighs like a second skin—and suddenly she found her throat too constricted to speak.

"Eliza." He shifted, his big body and the scent of brandy mixing with his earthy masculine essence nearly made her swoon. "Have I done something to offend you or upset you?"

Nothing—save to make me commit the horribly foolish mistake of falling in love with you.

She shook her head.

Marcus frowned and finished off his brandy. "Damnation," he muttered softly. His speech was turning a bit slurred. "If you insist on talking in business terms, let me say that I hope we can come to some other arrangement than simply employer and employee."

His dark eyes were now shrouded in shadow, making them impossible to read. "That is, a more intimate understanding between us."

Her emotions were already unsettled, but his oblique words caused her heart to skip a beat.

Was he suggesting that she become his mistress?

Blinking back tears, Eliza stepped back. "No doubt there are legions of ladies who would find such an offer enticing, milord. But I am not one of them."

"Eliza, you—"

"Please, sir," she interrupted, before he could go on. "This conversation is unwelcome and unwanted. I know my recent actions have made me appear rash and reckless, but I have not lost all sense of right and wrong."

His brow furrowed. "I—I don't understand…"

"Then let us leave it at that." Hugging her arms to her chest, hoping to hold what little dignity she had left, Eliza quickly skirted around him and hurried for the door. "Good night, milord."

* * *

"Bloody Hell." Marcus jabbed a poker into the glowing coals and stirred them to life. After adding several fresh logs to the fire, he slumped into the nearby armchair and took his head in his hands. His wits were a bit fuzzed from the brandy— but not fuzzed enough that he didn't recognize what a hash he had made of the encounter.

Cursing his stupidity, he stared blankly at the wagging tongues of flame, each one seeming to whisper a silent reproach for his clumsy words.

Had Eliza really thought he was offering her a tap on the shoulder?

A ragged sigh slipped from his lips. She had little reason to think otherwise, he admitted, given the way he had recently pawed over her glorious body and ravaged her lush mouth. Self-loathing squeezed at his chest, and for a moment, Marcus was tempted to drown his sorrows in another generous splash of brandy.

But some shred of sense remained, and he stayed seated, hoping the bright blaze of the burning logs might help dispel his black mood.

Love. He had been delighted by Lucien's announcement. Seeing the young couple flushed with such happiness had been heartening, and he was sure the match would flourish. But as he had watched Eliza throughout the meal, his spirits had plummeted. She looked so serious, so solemn. He didn't doubt that she approved, too. No, it hadn't been disapproval in her eyes, but rather a certain sense of longing.

Had she been in love and suffered a disappointment? he wondered.

The thought made him itch to bloody the offending fellow's nose—and then take Eliza in his arms and kiss the look of hurt from her face.

"But she doesn't want your kisses," he muttered to himself.

What a mull! She seemed to think he had been annoyed at having to rescue her from Hastings. When in fact, his heart had nearly stopped beating when he saw the knife pressed to her throat.

Love. Eliza might not have pulled the trigger of her ancient pistol, but she had managed to shoot Cupid's arrow deep into his flesh. Yes, he loved her, but as she didn't seem to return the sentiment, he would simply have to yank out the barb, no matter how much it hurt.

With that depressing thought in mind, Marcus rose and headed upstairs to his bedchamber. But he doubted that sleep would come anytime soon.

* * *

A SOFT KNOCK ON HER DOOR ROUSED ELIZA FROM HER brooding reveries. It was followed by Meredith's muffled half whisper.

"Are you awake?"

Much as she wished to be alone, Eliza didn't have the heart to ignore the query. Tightening the sash of her wrapper, she rose from the cushioned window seat and clicked open the latch. "Of course—who could possibly sleep, what with all the excitement bubbling through the manor house?"

Her sister smiled. "You are right to tease me, for no doubt I have been acting like a silly, moonstruck schoolgirl all evening. But I can't help it, I feel as if I am floating on a cloud of spun-silver starlight."

"As well you should." Eliza enveloped Meredith in a fierce hug. "If there is anyone who deserves to be happy, it is you."

"I *am* happy," answered Meredith. "Deliriously so. And I just wanted to share the moment with you, just the two of us, before retiring."

"I am glad you did," she murmured.

The two of them stood with their arms around each other for a sisterly interlude, no words necessary to express their feelings for each other.

"Dear me," Eliza finally broke away and dabbed her sleeve to her cheek. "With all this overflowing joy, I fear I am in danger of turning into a watering pot."

Meredith let out a soulful sigh. "I never dreamed such joy was possible. Lucien is so kind, gentle, caring, compassionate—"

"You need not exhaust yourself reciting all his sterling qualities," interrupted Eliza with a fond laugh. "I am in complete agreement that he is worthy of your hand."

"Thank you," said Meredith quietly.

"Not that it would make a whit of difference if I didn't approve," she added dryly.

Amusement sparkled in her sister's eyes. "You know me too well. But I never doubted that you would perceive the goodness in him. You have always been a very good judge of character."

Eliza gave an inward wince. "I do, on occasion, make mistakes," she murmured.

"Yes, but you're always wise enough to see the error of your ways." Meredith took a seat on the edge of the bed and smoothed at her skirts. "Take the earl…"

She closed her eyes for an instant, trying not to imagine his chiseled face dappled in red-gold firelight.

"The two of you—"

"This evening is all about you and your betrothed, not me and my employer," interjected Eliza.

"My happiness is assured," said Meredith. "Now it is your turn."

"What makes you think I am not happy?" she demanded. "I have my work, I have my independence, I have you and Mama, and the prospect of being a doting aunt."

Meredith dismissed the listing with a scornful snort. "Don't think to gammon me. As if I can't tell that you have something weighing on your spirits."

"Perhaps I do," she admitted. "But I am not ready to talk about it, if you don't mind."

"You don't have to," murmured Meredith. "I think I can guess what is troubling you, but since you have asked, I shall stay silent on the matter for now—save for one observation." She slid down from her perch. "Reason and logic are all very well, but sometimes it is better to listen to your heart, and not your head."

"I'm afraid both of them are speaking gibberish at the moment," quipped Eliza.

"Oh, I think Love has a very clear voice. You just have to listen very carefully to hear it."

Love.

She swallowed the rising lump in her throat, unable to think of a clever retort.

Meredith planted a quick kiss on her cheek. "Good night. And sweet dreams."

As the door clicked shut, Eliza blew out the candles with a heavy sigh, enveloping herself in the black velvet shadows of midnight. Sweet dreams were for couples whose hearts were joyfully entwined.

Her own reveries promised to be naught but a dark tangle of confusion.

Seventeen

Drawing a deep breath, Marcus crossed the garden terrace and descended the stairs to the sloping lawns leading down to the lake. He felt like Hell—a myriad of tiny devils seemed to be jabbing red-hot pitchforks into the back of his skull—but perhaps a brisk walk in the bracing air would help clear his head.

An early morning mist lingered in the rising sunlight, shrouding the trees and hedges in a silvery shimmer. The grass was damp with dew, muffling his steps as he made his way past the herb garden. Somewhere close by, a morning dove was twittering a soft song.

The sound made him wince.

"Damnation," he muttered, pressing his fingertips to his throbbing temples.

The pounding became more pronounced as a cheerful whistling cut through fluttering leaves.

Beethoven's Ode to Joy.

He didn't need to turn around to know who was approaching.

"You're up early, Uncle Marcus," called Lucien. "A lovely morning for a walk, isn't it?"

He grunted in reply, hoping the accompanying scowl would encourage his nephew to go away. Given his current mood, a besotted lover was the last sort of company he wanted.

But Lucien seemed oblivious to the message. Falling in step beside him, the young man fixed him with a quizzical look. "You look a little peaked. Is something amiss?"

Marcus bit back a caustic reply. No need to snap at those around him because of his own foul humor.

Lucien's brows rose a notch, but he refrained from further questions. "Fresh air, mellow sunshine, vigorous exercise," he murmured. "I always find that problems tend to untangle when one does not keep them cooped up in a deep, dark hole."

As their steps rounded the orchard fence, his nephew suddenly left off the Beethoven's melody to give three sharp whistles.

"Do stop that infernal racket," growled Marcus.

"Sorry." Lucien paused to greet his hound, who had come bounding out of the bushes with his tail wagging—and tongue lolling.

Marcus didn't react quite quickly enough to evade Ajax's muddy-pawed jump and slobbering kiss.

"Sorry," repeated his nephew, smothering a grin.

Looking down at his bedraggled breeches, he chuffed a reluctant laugh, feeling it would be churlish to stay all snaps and snarls in the face of such high spirits.

"Forgive me for not being in a more playful frame of mind," he said, ruffling his fingers through the hound's silky fur. "I don't wish to be like a stormcloud, scudding in on an ill-wind to darken your day. So perhaps it is best if you—and the Maestro's magnificent music—go on along this path, and I shall cut back through the copse of oak trees."

"Ah, is that because you wish to sulk through the shadows?" asked Lucien.

"As a matter of fact, yes." Marcus started walking away. "The sun is making my head ache."

"My guess is it's not the sun, or the moon, or the stars," called his nephew. "It's fear."

He stopped and slowly turned. "I beg your pardon?"

"Fear," repeated Lucien doggedly.

Ajax let out a little *woof*.

"What are you afraid of?" continued his nephew. "The fact that Miss Kirtland might say yes?"

Marcus stood still as a statue, fixing Lucien with a basilisk stare of silent shock and consternation. The young man didn't bat an eye.

"She won't," he finally said, his voice barely louder than a whisper. "Not after the hash I made of things last night."

"Would you care to talk about it?"

"No." Marcus quirked a wry grimace. "But that would be rather cowardly, considering the fact that I held your feet to the flaming coals."

"Trial by fire," quipped Lucien. "If you survive, you do tend to come out stronger."

"Thank you for the encouraging words," he replied dryly. "I've been roasting myself all night, and I can't say it's made me feel anything other than burned to a crisp."

Lucien approached, and after a quick glance at coal-black shadows under the earl's eyes, he took his uncle's arm and led him to the path that wound through the grove of trees. "You're right—you're not quite ready to greet the sun this morning. But perhaps I can help you see the light."

Bemused by this new steely show of confidence in his nephew, Marcus let himself by guided beneath the fluttering canopy of leaves.

"So, you think you've made a muddle of things with Miss Kirtland?" asked Lucien.

He nodded. "A hopeless muddle. She thinks I'm a scoundrel."

"Then change her mind."

Woof.

"I..." He found himself faltering. "I'm not sure I can."

"Oh, show some bottom, Uncle Marcus. Ye gods, if *I* can manage to win the hand of the lady I love, so can you."

Marcus blinked, then felt a smile curl on his lips. "You think so?"

"I know so. Meredith and I are quite sure that Miss Kirtland's heart is yours, if only you will ask for it."

"Ha." He expelled a harried sigh. "I started to, but she misunderstood—"

"So go back and try again," cajoled Lucien. "Or would the Black Cat rather slink away with his tail between his legs."

"Ouch," he murmured. "Since when have you developed such teeth and claws?"

"Since a certain someone challenged me to be more than I believed I could be."

Crunch, crunch. As their steps moved through the dead leaves on the path, Marcus felt new hope bloom in his heart. "She might not listen," he mused. "She's stubborn and willful." A laugh. "But so am I."

"You see—you are exceedingly well-matched." Lucien picked up a stick and tossed it into the trees. As Ajax went bounding after it, he added, "I think you would regret it for the rest of your life if you don't dare to go after her and make her say yes. Love is worth the risk."

Love. That word again. It was terrifying, and yet it was also...

Marcus stopped abruptly. "I think I shall leave you here and return to the manor. I have much to accomplish this morning and would prefer not to waste any more time."

"But of course," murmured his nephew. "Good luck. But then again, the Black Cat is accorded to be a very lucky feline."

"Yes, well, let us hope my luck holds."

* * *

Eliza looked around her familiar workroom in Rose Cottage and then took a seat at her desk. She aligned her pens in a neat row beside the inkwell. She straightened the stack of ledgers and squared the sheaf of foolscap. Everything was in its place, she thought as she stared down at her blotter. And like the blank sheets of paper, her life was ready to write a new chapter.

Turning to a fresh page.

In another week or two, once the earl has procured a special license and the marriage ceremony is over, she would be returning here, to her old familiar things.

Her old, familiar life.

Eliza knew she ought to be feeling elated at the prospects for the future. Meredith was in alt over her coming nuptials with Lucien, and she had no doubt that the new couple would suit each other in every way. The young man had also made it clear that he meant to see to the care of Rose Cottage and her ailing mother. So she would no longer have to bear the financial burden of looking after her family.

Her worries lifted, her independence assured—what more could she want?

Tracing her fingertips in random circles across the well-worn blotter, Eliza told herself she now had the freedom to do exactly as she pleased.

So why did the prospect look as black as the blot of ink beneath her thumb?

With a flick of her hand, she knocked all the nibs askew. *Hell's bells.* Her feelings were refusing to line up as they should. That her old routine suddenly seemed so empty, so...

"Eliza?"

Blinking the wetness from her lashes, she slowly turned around.

"I saw the door open and thought I would stop in and check that nothing is amiss."

"No, Ned, everything is back to the usual," she replied, trying very hard to keep her voice from sounding hollow.

Her neighbor's brow furrowed. "Actually, a good deal has changed."

She managed a smile. "Yes—and no. My life shall go on much as before."

Her neighbor shuffled his feet. "As to that..." Fisting his cap, he cleared his throat. "Might I speak...as a friend, Eliza?"

"Why, of course, Ned. You know I respect your opinions." Her lips quirked. "Even if I don't always agree with them."

A ghost of a smile flitted across his features. "Aye, you do have a mind of your own."

"I take that as a compliment."

"It was meant as one." He was back to looking very serious. "I could add a number of others, but I am a simple man, not much given to flowery speech, so I shall come straight to the point. I should like to ask for your hand in marriage."

"Marriage?" Eliza gripped the back of her chair. Lud, her whole world seemed intent on turning topsy-turvy this morning. "This is rather sudden."

He nodded. "Forgive me for not wooing you with a more formal courtship, Eliza. But you must know I admire you, and given the circumstances—"

"What circumstances are those?" she asked softly.

"You know how people are. They gossip, and even though any sensible soul in these parts knows you are not guilty of any impropriety, there are some unpleasant things being said about you and the Earl of Killingworth." He shifted uncomfortably, his gaze dropping to the tips of his muddy boots. "To be blunt, your reputation has suffered, and so I thought it best to waste no time in offering you the protection of my name."

Eliza was not sure whether it was anger or embarrassment or compassion—or a sparking of all three—that had her cheeks afire. "That is thoughtful of you, Ned. But as I have never given a fig in the past for what people have said, I have no intention of letting current whispers upset me in the least."

"We would have a comfortable life, Eliza," he went on doggedly. "My farm is a modest one, but with the improvements you suggested it is turning more profit. And I respect your judgment and value your counsel. I think we should suit."

Her own gaze slanted back to her desk. "On paper it might appear a good match, Ned. But I cannot accept your kind offer."

"Why?"

"Because..." Eliza turned to face him. No matter how hard a task, she could not duck away from the truth. "Because I do not wish to marry for mere comfort or convenience. Because I would not truly make you happy. Because..."

The rest of the words died on her lips as the sound of bootsteps scuffed down the corridor.

"I had not realized you had company, Miss Kirtland." Marcus hesitated in the doorway, the capes of his coat flapping against the molding. His windblown hair curled around his ears, softening the planes of his face.

Her heart fluttered in her chest.

"I do hope I am not interrupting anything serious."

"No—" she began.

"Actually, I was asking Miss Kirtland to marry me," announced Ned with a scowl.

"Allow me to be the first to offer felicitations," drawled Marcus, his brows taking on a sardonic tilt.

The farmer's fists clenched at his sides. "How kind. I would rather you give me a bit of privacy, milord."

Eliza was finding it difficult to draw in a gulp of air. Why the two men had taken such a dislike to each other was a mystery to her, but their growls of animosity was rubbing her already sensitive nerves raw. She felt stripped of all dignity, like a bone being clawed over by two terriers.

Caught between that which she didn't want and that which she couldn't have—the irony of it was suddenly too much to bear.

"Stop it—both of you!"

The men fell silent, Ned looking earnest, Marcus looking...enigmatic. His amber eyes, half hidden by a shock of dark hair, flickered with an inscrutable light as he folded his arms across his chest.

"Please leave." She knew she sounded perilously close to bursting into tears and didn't care. "If you don't mind, I would like some time to myself, to put my things in order."

"Of course. Whatever you wish, Eliza. These have been terribly trying times for you." Ned shot a dark look at the earl. "I am not pressing you for an answer now. All I ask is that you will consider my proposal."

She nodded, not having the heart to tell him her answer would be the same whether she thought on it for a day or a decade.

Marcus stepped aside to let the farmer pass. He lingered, his hooded gaze not quite meeting hers. She couldn't help but notice the smudge of shadows beneath his eyes, as if he, too, had passed a night plagued by bad dreams.

Making herself look away, Eliza moved to the side table and began to sort through a stack of pamphlets. After several ticks of the mantel clock, she heard him retreat into the corridor and quit the cottage.

Tears prickled against her lids, but she blinked them away.

It was time to turn the page, she reminded herself as she moved on to the stack of books beside the pamphlets. And leave her girlish longings in the past.

* * *

AN HOUR LATER, AFTER NUMBLY MOVING HER WORK materials from one spot to another with no awareness of what she was doing, Eliza gave up trying to concentrate on agricultural treatises and accounting ledgers. Making her way to the kitchen, she took up a willow basket hanging on a peg by the back door and headed out to the herb garden.

Chamomile, thyme, rosemary—as she gathered a handful of cuttings, the soothing fragrances helped calm her unsettled spirits. Moving on to another section of greenery, she paused to finger a delicate plant—

"Arnica for healing bruises."

Eliza spun around. "I—I am surprised you have learned something of medicine, sir."

"I have learned a great deal about a variety of subjects over the last few weeks," replied Marcus.

Eliza didn't reply, but broke off a twig of juniper. The tangy pine scent filled her lungs. It was, she knew, reputed to lift the spirits.

So why was it was only making her feel more blue-deviled?

It might have something to do with the earl's closeness, she admitted, and his own subtle male essence.

"Don't," he murmured, stepping closer.

Confused, she looked up from crushing the needles between her fingers.

"Don't marry him."

"W-why shouldn't I?" she whispered.

"Because you won't be happy," he answered.

That he was echoing her own feelings made her feel even more miserable.

"What you really mean is, he won't be happy with me." Eliza scraped a sleeve across her eyes. "You are right. Who would want to marry an aging, opinionated shrew?"

His mouth gave an odd little twist. "Me."

For an instant she thought the mockingbird's twitter was playing a teasing game with her. But the rippling in his amber eyes made her breath catch in her throat.

"I...I am not sure you have thought this out clearly," she croaked. "When you add up all the differences between us—"

Marcus placed a finger to her lips, silencing her stammering. "I have become very good at mathematics," he murmured. "For I've had a most excellent teacher."

His touch lit a spark of hope in her chest.

"Yes, we have our differences and our flaws. But when you add up the things that really matter—friendship, trust..." He swallowed hard, "...and most of all, love, the answer seems very clear. We are good for each other, Eliza."

At that moment, even a croak seemed beyond her power. Her throat was too tight.

"I love you," said Marcus. "I love your strength, your intelligence, your compassion, your courage." His expression turned oddly vulnerable. "Dare I hope you could learn to love a reformed rascal? For I am reformed, thanks to your help, and will do my best to always be worthy of your regard."

Eliza placed her palm against his stubbled cheek, reveling in the warmth that suffused her skin. "Your worth is beyond words, Marcus. You are strong, honorable, kind, humble—"

"I though you considered me arrogant," he murmured.

"Well, yes, you are at times. But I've come to find that rather endearing." Eliza slid her arms around his shoulders and hugged him tightly. "Surely you must know that I've loved you for an age."

"My arithmetic is sharp, but apparently I don't read hearts very well."

"We shall both work on that skill," she replied.

"Together, I hope," he said.

"Together," she agreed as his lips found hers.

"I trust that is a "yes" to my marriage proposal," whispered Marcus when finally he broke off the kiss.

"You haven't made one yet," said Eliza.

"Let me think of a suitably flowery one." He took his time in kissing her again. "Will you marry me?"

Eliza smiled. "On one condition."

His brows rose.

"I continue to have a role in managing the estate."

Amusement danced his eyes. "You drive a hard bargain."

"That's why you hired me," she responded. "So, do we have a deal?"

"Yes—if you will seal it with a kiss."

"Mmmm," Eliza gave a last little nibble to his lip, then eased back from his embrace. "I have to teach you to be a tougher negotiator."

"I am always open to learning new things from you, my love."

"And I from you," said Eliza, hugging him close.

"I think we shall make a perfect partnership." He paused. "No more pistols at dawn. The next time you are angry with me, we may discuss the matter over breakfast."

"No more pistols at dawn," agreed Eliza. "The coming days will be much too filled with sunlight to darken them with gunpowder."

Marcus drew her into a long, leisurely embrace before expelling a sigh. "Lovely as it is to linger here, we should probably return to the Manor and announce our news to the other betrothed couple."

"Somehow, I don't think they are going to be surprised. I think they recognized our true feelings long before we did." Eliza smiled. "In her own quiet way, Meredith gave me quite a scold last night."

"And Lucien rang a peal over my head this morning," admitted Marcus.

"That's because he loves you, and wishes to see you happy."

"Love," he mused, his gaze following the lazy spin of a rose petal caught in the gentle breeze. "Love can take the most unpredictable turns and come upon you when you least expect it."

Eliza twined her fingers with his and brushed a kiss to the back of his hand. "Unexpected love may be the sweetest of all. Just think of all the heartfelt bonds that now weave us all together—Lucien, Meredith, you, me."

"What I think," said Marcus as he encircled her in his arms, "is that the Black Cat has been transformed by love into the luckiest man alive."

Also by Andrea Pickens

TRADITIONAL REGENCIES

INTREPID HEROINES

The Banished Bride

The Storybook Hero

Second Chances

A Stroke of Luck

A Lady of Letters

The Defiant Governess

The Major's Mistake

The Hired Hero

Pistols At Dawn

DANGEROUS LIASIONS

A Diamond in the Rough

Sweeter than Sin

Devil May Care

REGENCY SPY/ADVENTURE/ROMANCES

MRS. MERLIN'S ACADEMY FOR EXTRAORDINARY YOUNG LADIES

The Spy Wore Silk

Seduced by a Spy

The Scarlet Spy

To Love a Spy

OTHER

Omnibus

Christmas by Candlelight

I started creating books at the age of five, or so my mother tells me. And she has the proof—a neatly penciled story, the pages lavishly illustrated with full color crayon drawings of horses and bound with staples—to back up her claim. I have since moved on from Westerns to writing about Regency England (clearly I have a thing for Men In Boots!) a time and place that has captured my imagination ever since I opened the covers of Jane Austen's "Pride and Prejudice."

I have a BA and an MFA in Graphic Design from Yale University, where I studied book design (As you see, I've always had a left brain-right brain love affair with art and the printed word.) These days, when I'm not tethered to my keyboard I enjoy traveling to interesting destinations around the world—however, my favorite spot is London, where the esoteric museums, funky antique markets and used book stores offer a wealth of inspiration for my stories.

OLIVERHEBERBOOKS

A small press bound by the belief that every voice matters.

Sign up for our newsletter to learn about new releases and more.
https://oliver-heberbooks.com/subscribe/

Follow us on social media:

facebook.com/oliverheberbooks

instagram.com/oliverheberbooks

amazon.com/oliverheberbooks

youtube.com/@OliverHeberBooksPublisher